THE AIRLINE PIRATES

Boysie Oakes, ex anguished agent, ex defective private
eye, greying horrifically at the temples, facing the
wilderness of middle-age under the Welfare State : and
the Welfare State cannot keep Boysie in the manner to
which, over the years, he has become accustomed.
Depression and gloom. Every time Boysie turns on the
television there is a play about some poor sod like him,
walled up in a bed-sitter with his sex life limp as an
empty banana skin, and a failing bank balance.
But Boysie, still terrified of life, has an urge to spit back
at bureaucracy. At long last he has reached seedy
maturity. Then, like an evil genie, up pops his oily old
boss, Mostyn, offering a life flowing with goodies.
Boysie is to become the sole British Director of Air
Apparent, an airline which operates from one office, has
no aircraft, yet, by juggling with officialdom and illegally
chartering aeroplanes manages to transfer its customers
to their destinations at half the scheduled fares and still
makes a vast profit.
Another bonus comes in triplicate, Air Apparent's three
wholesome hostesses, Aida, Ada and Alma. Boysie soon
finds that the business world is more of a jungle than
the complicated political East-West scene, while mild
people like the Board of Trade and the Ministry of
Transport and Civil Aviation have claws as sharp as the
KGB. But when Boysie discovers that Air Apparent is
being used for more nefarious purposes, such as the
shipment of arms to emergent nations, he is forced to
call in his old shooting partner, Charlie Griffin. Events
crowd in, culminating in hijacking, hilarity and, naturally,
hectic hedonism.

The Airline Pirates

A new Boysie Oakes adventure

John Gardner

CORONET BOOKS
Hodder Paperbacks Ltd., London

Printed in Great Britain
for Coronet Books, Hodder Paperbacks Ltd.,
St. Paul's House, Warwick Lane, London, E.C.4,
by Richard Clay (The Chaucer Press), Ltd.,
Bungay, Suffolk

ISBN 0 340 15954 5

The history of British legislation on this subject illustrates not only how wide a range of crimes may be assimilated to piracy by municipal law but also that nice questions of jurisdiction may arise.

D. P. O'Connel: *International Law*

Pan Am Makes The Going Great; Try A Little VC TENderness; and any other assorted commercials, particularly *It's Quicker By Air.*

Extract from *WHO'S WHO*

MOSTERVALE, Rear Admiral Sir Richard, K.B.E., *cr.* 1952; C.B. 1949; M.V.O. 1936; *b.* 22 August 1900; *s.* of Admiral Eversliegh Mostervale and Georgina Nellie (*née* Truecott); unmarried. *Educ.* R.N. College, Dartmouth. H.M.S. Ceres 1918-22; Portsmouth, Special Duties 1923-35; Admiralty 1935-39; Executive Officer Combined Operations (I) 1942-45; Captain 1944; Admiralty 1945-57; Rear Admiral 1951; Reserve List 1957; Attached as head of a department at Foreign Office 1958-67; Retired List 1967. *Recreations:* imbibology, art and opera. *Clubs:* Whites, Army and Navy. *Address:* 12 Abbot's Mews, W.8.

MOSTYN, Colonel Hon. James George, C.M.G. 1966; C.B.E. 1958; M.C. 1942; *b.* 4 March 1914; *s.* of The Hon. George Edward Mostyn and Alice May (*née* Longbow); unmarried. *Educ.* Haileybury College and New College, Oxford. Foreign Office 1935-38; attached 2nd Lancers 1939; Special Operations Executive 1941-46; Colonel on attachment 2nd Lancers 1947; Foreign Office, Special Consultant (Europe) 1949-58; Deputy Head of a department at Foreign Office 1958-67; Reserve List 1967. *Recreations:* Shooting, Golf. *Club:* Guards. *Address:* c/o Coutts & Co., 440 Strand, W.C.2.

12 Abbot's Mews
London,
W 8
01-937 1789

Dear Mostyn,

I suggest you get in touch with
me soonest. Most important suggestion
for you. To mutual advantage.

Sincerely,

Richard Mostervale

Foreign and Commonwealth Office
London S.W.1

TO: The Prime Minister.
FROM: The Foreign Secretary.
Date: 3rd March 1970
Index Code: A/4025/18

Dear Harold,

      Regarding the matter of President Anthony and
General Bushway about which we spoke on Thursday last.

      I am pleased to inform you that the officer who
appraised me of the latest situation has now been put in full
control of what he likes to call 'his own outfit'.

      I have given him a free hand. DI 5 and our own IS
have been fully acquainted but will remain in reserve, though
some individual members are involved.

      I have complete confidence that, in this way,
the whole matter will be dealt with in a manner that does
not openly involve HM Government or Forces.

        Yours cordially,

        Michael

        Foreign Secretary

1

IT WAS THE moment he had dreaded: the fraction of time we all spend our lives trying to prevent. Now there was no avoiding it. The moment of truth.

The big white Ford GT40 reversed, lining up and pointing its nose directly at him with uncompromising accuracy. But he remained paralyzed.

The car moved, beginning to build up speed. Closer. Tyres singing. Straight. He did not even brace himself. Now. It was going to hit . . . hit . . . hit . . .

The battery-operated model thudded against Boysie Oakes' right shoe and was deflected, whirring off across the carpet.

It was a clever toy which worked by feeding a programmed card into the underside of the model. The edges of the card could be cut so that, as it moved through a pair of rollers, it connected with spring-loaded buffers, pushing them apart or closing them, thereby controlling gears and steering.

In theory you could cut the card and make the car drive itself all round the room without hitting anything. Highly instructional. A child of ten could do it. Boysie often found that children of ten were more advanced with things like that. He found it difficult to make the wretched thing drive away from him, stop, reverse and return so that it missed the chair on which he was sitting.

He had bought the car in a moment of exhilaration last Christmas while the brandy-breathed Santas were conning the toddlers. The moment had come, in the toy department of the big store, at the same second as a dazzling smile from a chick all done up in a little black dress, the kind they made them wear to work in big stores.

She was around eighteen with a waist so tiny that Boysie

knew he could just open up his big hands and make the tips of his thumbs and forefingers touch, with room to spare, if he encircled it.

But that was a dream, living on for a precious five seconds in the middle of all the clamour and hell-raising of a merry Christmas spend up.

The smile had cost Boysie a couple of quid for the toy car which he promptly stowed away for a rainy day and only remembered again now, on this blustery March night, and he was damned if he could work the thing properly.

Boysie was bored. He had been bored for the best part of a year : ever since the private security organisation, Grimobo, founded by his ex-boss, Colonel James George Mostyn, had succumbed to the credit squeeze of the late sixties.

Still with a little capital left, Boysie had moved from the comparative splendour of Dolphin Square to more modest surroundings at the better end of the Earl's Court Road. *1 bedr'm, 1 stng. rm, ktn, bt'rm.* It was not luxury, but it left a little spare cash for things like food and drink.

He crossed the room, pulled back the curtains and stared down into the street, watching the little bundles of living jumble trudge along damp pavements. Across the road there was a family-size double-fronted shop. *Newsagent S. W. Wood Tobacconist.* In its small doorway a man strained his eyes to read the postcard ads. The man was wearing a grey raincoat.

Boysie allowed the curtain to drop, turned back into the room and switched on the television, slumping into a chair and lighting a cigarette. Slowly the picture emerged. It showed a junk-ridden room with a bed, rear centre. On the bed lay a middle-aged woman apparently garbed in rags. Forward, and to the right, was a table. At the table sat a middle-aged man. He wore a stained striped shirt without a collar, and a pair of trousers with a large rent in the left leg. His hair, what was left of it, stuck matted to a dirty scalp.

"Noel Coward," observed Boysie.

He leafed through the *Evening Standard* to find the TV Guide. "Ah! The Wednesday Play. *The Glittering Gem* by Sam Cole." It looked as gripping as a wet lettuce.

The man on the screen was indulging himself in a ferocious

bout of coughing. The coughing eased and he took a deep breath, launching into conversation with the lady on the bed. The matted, coughing man spoke first.

You didn't get the cocoa then?

What cocoa?

The cocoa you usually get before we go to bed.

I don't usually get the cocoa. You get it. You usually get the cocoa. Ten o'clock. You get the cocoa.

Never. If I get it then I get it at a quarter to ten. Now it's five past.

Argue. That's all we do. Sit here and argue. Day in day out. Month after month. Year by year. Seems there's no fun to life any more. There were days, long ago days, when we used to get out into the green fields where the birds sing in the sky and the wind sobs on the cheeks of cripples in consolation. But not any more.

We ain't got any cocoa anyway.

Why ain't we got none?

'Cos you didn't go and collect the benefit, did you?

Benefit? What do I want with benefit? Bloody charity. Bloody Welfare State's charity, we don't want none of that. Here I am, used to be able to work hard, earn a good honest wage and what am I reduced to now? A husk. A living shell. No work. No pleasure, not even with you in bed like we used, 'cos I lost me strength and when we do it's only pleasurable when you get a coughing spell. Look at me. Look at me.

The camera did as it was bidden and went into close-up. The ravaged face was horrific. The man went on.

And me only forty-eight.

"Oh Christ," said Boysie aloud, leaping for the set and switching off. "Forty-eight. Christ." He went into the bathroom, put the light on, and began to peer at his face in the mirror.

The hair was greyer and had receded a shade, but it was still a good strong face. Maybe the odd line or two now, but one had to expect that. The eyes, ice blue, remained as clear as ever. Who was he kidding? A year of doing nothing had sapped his strength. Too many cigarettes. Too many late nights and not enough exercise. It would not do. He decided that his body called for some form of stimulation. A walk. A walk to some hostelry, probably.

17

Boysie went over to the window again and looked into the street. The wind still blew but there was no rain. The man in the raincoat still stood in the doorway of *Newsagent S. W. Wood Tobacconist.*

Boysie shrugged into his short suede car coat with the fur collar. It was getting shabby, a small tear in the right shoulder, but it still kept out the cold from the knees upward.

The wind was strong when he hit the street. Strong and gusty, belching up from the cavern of Kangaroo Valley, the far end of the Earl's Court Road inhabited by Ned Kelly immigrant Australians who preferred the old country to the glare of Bondi Beach and all the Sheilas who spread themselves on the sand of the emigrate and prosper posters.

With the wind behind him, Boysie struck out in the direction of Kensington High Street.

Old habits die hard. With long accustomed care he glanced over his left shoulder as he turned into the High Street. The man in the grey raincoat was walking on the opposite side of the road but in the same direction.

Boysie slowed his pace, clenching his fists in the pockets of the car coat. This was not the first time. During the twelve months away from the frantic world, the nightmare land of security, he had suffered several uncomfortable moments: times when he imagined the past was edging back to meet him, or at least catch up with him.

There were many things about his past that Boysie Oakes would prefer to forget. Blood stained the memory as well as the hands.

He had gone a hundred yards up the High Street before he was certain that Grey Raincoat was tailing him. A quick dead feeling in the stomach and that arid sensation at the back of the throat told him he was unhappy about the situation.

Give him a run for his money, he thought and walked on, conscious of the soundless footsteps behind him.

He kept the pace steady and slow. There were not many people about and if the tail was out for a kill it could be done quickly with an easy getaway. Boysie was not anxious to force that kind of issue by breaking into a run.

He got to the entrance of Kensington High Street tube station before making a move. Two steps past the entrance he suddenly spun round and moved fast down the alleyway, running for the ticket machines.

For a second he wondered if it had been a wise choice. There were still too few people about. He banged a tenpenny piece into a machine, grabbed at his ticket and headed towards the trains.

There were four people on the platform. A couple intent on public copulation. A young lad surreptitiously filling in some detail on a corset advertisement, and an elderly man in the London businessmen's uniform. It was cold and draughty, backed by the odd sounds of underground stations. A minute went by. Grey Raincoat had not appeared. From far away came the first whine of an approaching train. Boysie stood close to the wall, his eyes fixed on the platform entrance. The train was louder. Nearer. Still no raincoat.

The rattling silver and glass capsule came rushing in, opening its doors with an electric grumble. The other four passengers climbed aboard. Boysie still waited, eyes flicking between the entrance and the compartment doors in front of which he had positioned himself.

The doors gave their pre-shutting sigh and he dived towards them into the compartment. As he ran the five or so paces the agony leaped in the pit of his stomach. On the periphery of his vision Boysie caught the flash of grey moving from the entrance to the train. As he leaped aboard he turned. There was time enough to see that the raincoat had also boarded the train.

Boysie fell into a seat on the far side. The compartment was empty except for a painted lady who moved as the train began to roll. She walked the length of the compartment, sat down next to Boysie and enquired if he had a light, holding up a battered Grosvenor as though it was vital evidence.

Without speaking he dug into the inside pockets of his jacket and extracted a tin of Benson and Hedges and the heavy gold Dupont lighter, which long ago had replaced his battered Windmaster with the unfortunate monogram *BO*.

He carefully removed a cigarette, placing it between his

lips before clicking up the lid of the lighter and flicking his thumb, all in one movement like a Western sharpshooter. The flame glowed and he offered it to the painted lady. She was of uncertain age and, judging by the bone structure, capricious breeding. She thanked him for the light and, as he kindled his cigarette, asked him if he fancied something different.

Boysie looked hard at her with his ice blue eyes and smiled. The smile was attractive. It was also lopsided, curving up the left side of his lips. He inhaled deeply on the smoke and blew it out in a long stream. "What you got, lady? Typhus?" was what he wanted to ask.

"No thank you. Not tonight," was what he actually said before returning to the problem of Grey Raincoat. By the time he had worked it out they were pulling into Gloucester Road.

The painted lady disembarked and Boysie moved towards the doors, not going too close. Once more he waited until the last possible moment. The mechanism signalled its action with the usual telltale sigh but he remained immobile until the doors actually began to move together before pushing himself through sideways onto the platform and away up the steps, waving his ticket at the collector at the barrier; now fast to the right. Up the second flight of steps and into the lift.

There were two other people already in the big double-ended elevator and he could hear steps of more approaching. Boysie turned away, sneaking looks over his shoulder.

Two women. No Grey Raincoat.

The lift door slid, tonging shut and they slowly dropped, back into London's bowels.

At the bottom, Boysie was off again at speed, through the tunnels to the Piccadilly Line.

Grey Raincoat was not behind. Boysie was away and safe.

He walked right up to the far end of the platform feeling contented with his good fortune. It was not until the train came in and he was settled in his seat that he began to search more deeply into the situation.

Grey Raincoat had been staking him out. He had undoubtedly tailed him. Why? It had to be something to do with his past: either the long years he had spent as Liquidator to the government controlled Department of Special Security, or the short and fatuous time, following the Department's disbandment, when he had been with Mostyn in Grimobo.

The Liquidator bit was the most likely. He had made plenty of enemies then. Towards the end too many people had known. These boys were like gun dogs and they knew where to find him. He could not go home.

The future looked decidedly wintery. He did not have to look in his wallet or pockets to know what the financial situation was. He carried five pounds ten shillings and his cheque book. There was just under a thousand left in the bank and only yesterday he had seriously considered the possibility of work. If that was not a gloomy enough thought there was now the indisputable fact of violence at his shoulder. And he could not go home.

He did not get off at South Kensington or Knightsbridge; nor at Hyde Park Corner or Green Park. Boysie just sat there staring into space, greatly troubled and remembering what life on the run was like. Dirty cheap hotels. Hideaway cafés. Chicks are not chicks any more. Grease. Sludge tea. Railway stations and grimy second class carriages. Second class everything. Then the money would run out and there would be nothing but the open air, the cold and the soaking rain.

He wondered, for ten seconds, if he should make a run for it. Into the country; the cottage he had always wanted. Hell, all that fresh air; he could not live in the country any more. His childhood memories of the Berkshire Downs were enough. That was all soft nostalgia now. He had the creeping cramps in the guts but the years were responsible for a change. He could still get bloody frightened but he was harder inside. The train stopped. Piccadilly. Let's have a a look at the bright lights and see what the hippies aren't doing tonight.

Out onto the platform and Boysie's bowels did their inimitable head roll. Grey Raincoat was ahead of him walking up the platform fifteen yards in front.

Boysie slowed in order to allow his thinking processes time

to react. He could not go home. Grey Raincoat was in front of him. He did not know why he was being followed in the first place. He now had the upper hand. Go in and find out what it is all about.

He kept his distance, closing only as they got near the final exit barrier so that three people separated him from Grey Raincoat.

Then they were out in the crowded circular concourse of Piccadilly Underground Station and Grey Raincoat was headed for the telephone booths.

As usual they were all occupied and he had to stand there waiting. Boysie moved up behind him, swallowed, stuck one hand in his coat pocket and walked right up beside him, jabbing a forefinger into the man's side.

"I am not joking. This is a Smith and Wesson Chiefs Special. I only tell you the manufacturer so you'll know it can make a nasty mess of your raincoat as well as your kidneys. Your quest is over."

"What quest?" He tried to put a laugh in it.

"For the holy grail. You just found it."

"The holy grail?"

"Me. I'm the holy grail. The name's Oakes. Brian Ian Oakes, known to his confidantes as Boysie."

"So?"

"So you've spent the evening watching my pad and following me."

"Have I?"

"You know bloody well you have." This was getting a little difficult. The rigid finger bit right out in the open was the kind of thing liable to attract attention. He decided to increase the pressure. "I want to know who sent you and why. I shall count three. If you don't render the info I shall make this firestick speak with leaden tongue and you'll be spread all over the concrete."

"And you'll be none the wiser."

"The one who takes your place will talk. Or the one after him. They'll have to be good. I was on to you sharp enough."

"Bloody sharp," growled Grey Raincoat. "I bin watching you for a week."

"One . . ." said Boysie after a quick swallow following the last setback. "Two . . ."

"Okay, put down the shooter," mouthed Grey Raincoat. "You going to spill?"

"Better. I'll take you to him."

"Oh no. I want to know who and why."

"Well, I don't know who. Don't know his name, that is. And I don't know why. He just told me to follow you, watch you and make a report at the end of the week. That's tomorrow."

"What sort of report?"

"Usual. Who you're kipping with. Where you go. What you do. Financial status. Habits. You got some bad habits, haven't you mate?"

"Where's his drum?"

"He told me to ask you round if you gave me any aggro."

"Did he now? Okay. You go first, I'm right behind you."

They went up the exit steps on the corner of Regent Street opposite the Regent Palace, walked up the street and hailed a cab.

Grey Raincoat asked for an address in Hans Place just behind Harrods. In the taxi Boysie sat slewed over in one corner still keeping the fictitious gun on the man. He could see him properly now. Weasel-faced with slightly protruding teeth, yet quite well set up.

The house was converted into two flats.

"He's upstairs," Grey Raincoat told Boysie.

The entrance hall was plain but cared for. The door to the upstairs flat gleamed white. It also looked very solid. Boysie told his prisoner to push the bell. It took a long minute before the footsteps sounded and the key turned.

The door opened to reveal a short man, neatly dressed in conservative grey. His tight curly hair was now more grizzled than Boysie remembered.

"Well, well. Look what the ever-changing sea of life's washed up on me front doorstep. How are you, Boysie old laddie?" Mostyn grinned. It was the grin of a rat about to kill.

2

Six Scavenging Lizards rutted around in Boysie's stomach. Moments of sheer terror were not unknown to him, but the fear that his former boss, Mostyn, always produced was unique.

"I might have known," was all that Boysie could blurt.

"Come on, laddie. Only trying to help. You know your uncle Mostyn." He stood there, confident, the oily self-satisfied smile lubricating his face.

"Sorry about this, sir, I lost him on the tube then he got the better of me," said Grey Raincoat. "I should warn you he's armed."

Boysie felt better. He grinned, lifted his right hand and waggled his forefinger at Grey Raincoat. "Smith and Wesson Chiefs Special."

"Jesus," said Grey Raincoat.

"I warned you, Harold, Boysie boy's full of cheerful surprises. If you've nothing else to tell me perhaps you'd jog along. Call me tomorrow eh?"

"As you like. And the name's Albert."

Mostyn motioned Boysie inside and closed the door firmly. "A political pauper," he said, nodding to where Grey Raincoat had been left, blank-faced. "Real name's Albert Wilson. Hates me calling him Harold. Come and have a drink."

He led Boysie down the long hall and into a room decorated in warm shades of pink. It was a little chichi for Boysie but typical of sharp little, smooth little, and very professional little Mostyn.

"Sit down." Mostyn motioned to a deep easy chair. "You still drink brandy?"

Boysie nodded. "Who is he?"

"Who?" Mostyn asked from a long bottlescaped marble table.

"Harold. Albert. Wilson."

"Well he's not a government man."

"You could tell that. He didn't twitch. Look, this is bloody cheeky. You put him on to me, I'd like to know who he is and what game we are playing?"

Mostyn grinned his slippery grin and held out a large balloon glass containing a liberal quantity of the dark amber liquid.

"I don't play games, Oaksie. After all these years you should know that. I instigate games but I don't play them. Albert Wilson is an enquiry agent."

"A private detective."

"A good one."

"He was no good as a tail. I had him cold."

"Ah, but I trained you, didn't I? Cheers. To absent friends." Mostyn raised his glass. Boysie knew exactly who the absent friends were: the great army of dead whose lives had been forfeited during the multitude of games Colonel Mostyn had set in motion during his time as Second in Command of Special Security.

Boysie took a sip from the glass. The brandy caught his throat and exploded in a wall of flame against his guts. Spare cash had not been running to good brandy lately. The pain was exquisite.

"Why have me followed?" he asked once his breathing returned to normal and the tears were wiped from his eyes.

"Simply wanted to pick up old threads. Like to know if things have changed, especially when I'm considering making an offer to an old friend."

"An offer?" Boysie thought about the last sentence. An offer from Mostyn to an old friend was rather like handing out dishes of hemlock at a birthday party. Boysie pushed his tongue hard into his cheek and waited for around sixty seconds. "You look jolly well. Sunburnt and all that. Been in foreign parts?"

"Pretty foreign, laddie. South Africa."

"That must have been nice for you. You'd enjoy it out there. Suit your style. What were you at, hiring a labour force?"

Mostyn showed his teeth. "Enough lad," he hissed. "You can cool the clever chat and listen to me."

Boysie rose with what elegance he could muster. "I shall be leaving now."

"Sit down lad. I've got a proposition."

"I've thought about it. Your propositions are murder. I've no desire to get mixed up in business motivated by you. Never again."

"Sit down. I can help you. I also know far too much about you."

Boysie sat. "You don't change, do you?"

"For that you should be thankful. I well remember the day I walked into a dirty, stinking rotten third class café and offered you better things. You jumped at that. For all the bad moments you did discover that life could be pleasant without financial troubles."

"I can manage."

"After a fashion. You're not getting any younger, Boysie, and I can offer you a certain security."

"When you start checking up on someone and making propositions it means the job's dirty and, if necessary, you'll resort to blackmail as they used to say in B movies."

"If you'll just listen . . ."

"Hopeless . . ."

"I've found a licence to print money . . ."

"Ah." Boysie was hooked for a second. "No. No, I've made up my mind. I'm not going to get myself involved."

"Airlines."

"I don't hear you."

"Airlines carry people to and from places and they charge high prices."

"A lot of wind for this time of the year."

"What if I told you I've discovered a way to run an airline and make a profit by only charging half the normal fares?"

26

"It's against the law. They have rules to stop people doing that kind of thing. It's lawless. Unruly. Irresponsible. It's shifty."

"Quite. It shifts people in bulk from place to place. I have the capital."

"I dare say. You're well connected."

"Not my money, lad, you don't think I'd use my own money for a business venture?"

"Who's the sucker?"

"No sucker. Part of it was his idea. What if I tell you the Chief put up the bread."

"The Chief?" It was unthinkable. By the Chief, Mostyn meant the former Chief of Special Security, an elderly retired Admiral with a line of invective which could stop a flame-thrower, and an unquenchable thirst for Chivas Regal. As Chief of Special Security he had proved outstandingly incompetent: hence Mostyn's tremendous power in the Department before its discontinuance.

"Surprise you?" Mostyn leaned back in his chair, master of nearly all he surveyed.

"I suppose he's senile now."

"Far from it. Spends most of his time agitating against our masters."

Boysie still could not see it. The Chief and Mostyn were both, in his mind, synonymous with the Establishment. "What's the deal?" he asked, interested only in details.

Mostyn sipped his brandy. "We would run a nice comfortable airline." The voice was almost hypnotic. "A super office somewhere in the heart of London. Nice young girls to do your bidding, deal with the office chores, and double as ground hostesses when needed. Piped music, the best Musak can provide . . ."

"Cut the commercial. How does it work?"

"Like a super travel agency only we call ourselves an air company. We find enough people who want to go to a particular part of the globe for a more reasonable fee than they would have to pay a regular airline. We then charter an aeroplane for them as a group. Take them to the aircraft on the appointed day and wave them goodbye."

"And what would I do?" It was too easy. There had to be something.

"You would mind the store."

"And that would entail?"

"Hiring and firing of dollies. Advertising. Acting as go-between with the air charter company. Booking the ladies and gentlemen on their flights, and seeing that they all get aboard safely. You would also be required to wine and dine some people of influence when I'm not doing that. Oh, and you would be a director of the company."

"The fall guy. The patsy. What's wrong with all this, Mostyn? There must be a catch."

Mostyn smiled. A snake at rest.

"It's illegal, isn't it, for a start?"

"Yes. You could say that. But I would put it another way. It's illegal if you get caught and if they can prove anything. We would operate as a perfectly legitimate company."

"But it's a fiddle."

"A Stradivarius. You'd be very happy with us."

"Just a brace of questions." Boysie had a fair idea of what the job was now. Many years ago he had learned to read the strange and cryptic language spoken by Mostyn. When Mostyn smoothly offered you something that looked like a doddle it was invariably dangerous.

"Interrogate, dear boy. Interrogate, examine, be my inquisitor."

"These aircraft that are going to be magic carpets for the clients?"

"Yes?"

"Would I be expected to travel on them?"

"Under normal circumstances, no."

"And abnormal circumstances?"

Mostyn gave the matter five seconds' thought. "In the unlikely event, you might, just might, be asked to take a short trip."

Boysie nodded, narrowing his eyes in understanding. Mostyn knew that one of his pet hatreds was flying. "And what," he asked, "would be my magnificent salary?"

28

Mostyn chuckled, leaned forward and patted Boysie's knee in a knowing sort of way, then rose and stood by his chair looking at Boysie after the manner of a horse dealer.

"I suppose we'd have to kit you out first. You have got a shade rat-eaten, haven't you, laddie."

"Well?"

"Five hundred for clothes and grooming. Then, fifty quid a week after tax."

Boysie nodded. "No," he said loudly.

"You haven't got a driving licence for hard bargains, Oaksie. Tell you what; why don't you finish up your brandy, go home and think about it? Call me on Monday. My card." He held out the small oblong pasteboard which Boysie took and stuffed into his breast pocket.

"It's no good, Mostyn. You took a great hunk out of my life once before and made it agony. I'm not travelling your way again."

"It's the only way you'll ever travel first class. You want to remember that."

"I'll manage."

"At your age? And with your experience?"

Boysie did not want to think about it so he shut Mostyn's words away into the sealed section of his mind.

The electricity company sent a nice combined greetings and bill which arrived on the next morning. It was printed in red and informed Boysie that they would cut off the electricity if he did not settle the account within seven days.

The gas company sent a similar message by the lunchtime mail. There was also an odd assortment of incidental bills.

Boysie began to perform simple feats of mathematics which did not call for the eloquence of an abacus nor the complexities of a computer.

By Saturday he was making some attempt to face up to reality. His financial float had taken nearly all the punishment it could stand. The hard cash was running out. It was only a matter of time before some other form of income would have to be found.

On that Saturday evening Boysie took a deep breath and plunged out into the streets, heading for the West End. Oxford Street seemed more of a disaster than he remembered it: garish, cheap and plastic while the people had a brittle cold look about them as well. He trudged down Regent Street into Piccadilly which was equally smudged with despair. There was the sense of being near to something desperate, on the corner of apathy: the lethargy that touches a man trapped in intense cold and brings him into the freezing sleep.

The Faces floated past Boysie, either set and belligerent or pleading. Perhaps, he thought, it was himself: a shabbiness that had pervaded his own life for too long. Something had to be done about that for a start.

On the following afternoon he sat down to really think things out. Behind the present greyness there must be another kind of life. That was indisputable because once he had nearly touched it. Not a soft cloying and destructive luxury, but a way of life that paid off in self-respect.

His mind kept floating back to Mostyn's offer. There was a definite attraction. Money. But his old boss was not opening the doors to the past: leading him back to the strange under-cover world they had once both inhabited. This, Boysie told himself, was different. This was the world of big business. The Power Game. The Money Market.

Sitting by the window, dreaming as he looked down into the Earl's Court Road and across to *Newsagent S. W. Wood Tobacconist*, it was quite simple to propel himself through the glossy looking glass and the magazines of smooth and soothing texture. The office with its leather-buttoned chairs, the long desk, trim phones, trim secretary, a massive abstract on the wall and work flicked off with the nerveless assurance of a master tycoon.

The BAC contract, Stephanie?

Yes, Mr Oakes, ready in five minutes.

It'd better be, I have to catch the noon flight to New York for the meeting with Howard Hughes.

"Mr Midas," he muttered to himself. "Whizz Kid Operator Cleans Out The Market."

Across the road *Newsagent S. W. Wood Tobacconist* stood where it always stood. A brace of sheepskin rugs, topped with straggling long hair, plodded past, and a delicately poised young woman walked purposefully, tight white boots peeping from below her scarlet maxi coat as the traffic thickened, scenting the air with its particular pollution.

He turned from the window and switched on the eternal telly. A long-haired young man was being tedious and boring, telling four smooth prune-faced gentlemen that the stinking dirty capitalist society was tedious and boring and that he for one was not going to work for anyone ever again and there were thousands like him who would eventually bring the country to its knees. Two of the smooth prune-faced gents nodded rhythmically showing that they understood and sympathised. The other pair smiled superciliously.

Nobody, thought Boysie, bothered to point out that the long-haired young man was probably right and in about thirty years he would inherit the society of his choice. But by then youth would once more be having its fling.

On Monday, Boysie called Mostyn.

"I thought you'd see sense," said Mostyn.

"I haven't seen sense. But I want to talk with you. I need to know more."

"That means you're interested, lad. If you're interested you'll take the final step and join us. Come round and I'll disclose all."

Half an hour later, Boysie was sitting in Mostyn's lair clutching a glass of brandy.

"Well?" asked Boysie.

"My offer still stands. Plus a nice bonus." Mostyn smiled silkily.

"I simply want details. I haven't made a decision yet."

"Come on, Oaksie. You can't pick and choose. You're not a blunt instrument. You're not jolly James Bond."

"Neither was he."

Mostyn flashed his stiletto look and grunted. "You want to hear it?"

"As it is, without the frills and cons," said Boysie with a force that surprised even him.

31

Mostyn relaxed and stared into his glass. "Let's put it like this. To switch on to this scene you've got to understand the basic principles."

"Such as?"

"Such as we have everything set up to open a company under the brilliantly descriptive name AIR APPARENT."

Boysie pursed his lips and looked at Mostyn. "Your idea?"

"Naturally."

"That figures. And Air Apparent is an airline?"

"In a way. To start up an airline would be costly and not of great profit. Expensive things, aeroplanes."

"I can imagine."

"Then there's all that red tape about schedules and getting landing permits and routes. Very boring. Board of Trade regulations. Ministry of Transport and Civil Aviation."

"You don't want to bother with them?"

"Not if we can help it." Mostyn spoke slowly, clipping the words. "But we rather want to transport people across the world at a maximum profit with a minimum outlay and at the most attractive terms."

Boysie's brain was working slowly but steadily. "You mean that the people who want to travel have to be charged as little as possible?"

"In a nutshell, old Boysie. E for effort."

"I thought there was some regulation about that. All the airlines have to charge the same prices or something."

"Yes," Mostyn drawled unpleasantly. "That's another fly in the ointment. IATA."

"IATA?"

"International Air Transport Association."

"Who are they?"

"Top brass. Issue all regulations concerning commercial air transport. They're like a kind of governing body for the scheduled airlines. They also tell the scheduled airlines how much they must charge passengers."

"But there's a way round that?"

"Amazing." Mostyn beamed. "You catch on with great speed, laddie. Proud of you. Let me explain finances."

"Do. Do. Please do."

"If a scheduled airline is granted permission to fly a service to, say, Johannesburg in South Africa they have to charge a one-way fare, tourist class, of one hundred and fifty-nine pounds seventeen shillings." He sighed and shook his head. "Now a Boeing 707 carries around two hundred passengers, so, on a full one-way trip, there can be a passenger commitment of around fifty-two thousand pounds."

Boysie whistled long, low and in awe. "Some bread."

"Would it surprise you, my dear old laddie, if I told you we could charter a 707 to South Africa for around seven thousand pounds?"

"One way?"

"One way. With crew, handling, fuel, hostesses the lot. Seven thousand green ones."

"That means . . ."

"That means, laddie, that as long as we have a landing permit, and as long as we charter the aeroplane purely for the use of some club or organisation, we are home and dried."

Boysie was not quite with him, but nearly. "More," he said in the flat tone which Oliver Twist must have used.

Mostyn leaned forward in a conspiratorial fashion. "Air Apparent takes out a discreet advertisement offering a one-way trip to South Africa at sixty-nine pounds a head. We then charter an aeroplane telling the charter firm that members of the South African Free Swinging Polo Fanciers would like to return to their native shores. Each ticket we sell also provides instant membership of the SAFSPF back-dated six months to make it legal. If we sell all two hundred seats we take thirteen thousand eight hundred pounds. Deduct seven thousand for the hire of the aeroplane. Another eight hundred for our own running expenses, your salary, the secretaries, and we have a round profit of six thousand pounds." He paused to let it sink in. "If we have a similar operation running at the other end we make a total of twelve thousand pounds. One trip a month and a bonus for you of two-and-a-half grand a month. What do you say?"

"It's against the bloody law and you'll never get landing permits in South Africa."

"No? What about landing somewhere in Angola? Luanda has a good airport. Our passengers could catch regular scheduled flights from there to Jo'burg. No problem. Angola still belongs to Portugal. I know a man in Lisbon . . ."

"I'll bet you know a man in Lisbon. It's still against the law. It's bloody piracy."

"Yo-ho-ho and a magnum of Bollinger." Mostyn raised his glass. "Fifty quid a week and a quiet two-and-a-half grand a month just for running an office. Can't be bad."

"It's still piracy. How many regulations will you be breaking?"

"Around fifty-two. But don't let that worry your little head. Nobody's going to denounce us in Whitehall. Some of the best companies work this racket. We're only running a super travel agency after all."

"You mean I'll be running it. What happens if something goes wrong?"

Mostyn spread his hands wide. "What on earth can go wrong?"

"Hundreds of things. The whole idea's unpatriotic. I always thought you were a government man."

There was a spurt of aircraft noise from outside and above. As it died away the small man answered. "I've evolved a new philosophy, Boysie. Yes, I was a government man until they chucked me. Then Wilson's lot got to sniffing round my private concerns. I have ceased to trust *all* governments. They haven't done you much good either."

The past shrieked into Boysie's guts leaving an unpleasant tingle behind. Not just the immediate past of Special Security but the long past which he had managed to hide for decades. "What do you mean they haven't done me much good?"

Mostyn smirked. A man who knew much but was not going to talk. "What do you think? They chucked you, old son. There are other factors as well, aren't there?"

Boysie hammered down his emotions, closed his mouth and took a deep breath through his nose.

"Come on, Boysie. It would be a caper."

34

"What," began Boysie loudly, "would happen if we were caught infringing regulations?"

"Infringing regulations? You sound like some probationary constable. Been reading too many mediocre thrillers, lad. What would happen? A small fine, I should imagine. But let the Chief and I take care of all that. After all it's the Chief's money and my brains. I set it up: you do the front work, with the help of some scrumptious dollies of course."

It was a long time since Boysie had been near enough to a scrumptious dolly for him to tell if it mattered any more. Christ, he thought, I have gone stale: sour. He also needed the money. There was the other thing as well. The chance to hit back. The swift, sure kick right up the arse of bureaucracy. The pay-off for the death-rattling years while he had been a paid killer for the government, and the final screw for that buried debt never to be brought into the light.

Slowly he nodded. "All right. I'll be your man."

"Here's to the managing director of Air Apparent (London) Limited." Mostyn appeared transmogrified in Boysie's eyes. A rodent shining with health, eyes bright, teeth flashing as though he had just observed his favourite prey asleep and very vulnerable.

"Here's to Air Apparent and its London director." This time the beverage was champagne and it was the Chief who proposed the toast. He had changed little. The same florid complexion and bombast. "By Nefertiti's titties it's good to feel oneself back on the bridge. Bleedin' clever idea of Mostyn's, eh Oakes?"

Boysie woke from a small dream. He had been eyeing the photographs on the wall by the Chief's desk. The Chief with royal personages and officers under his command back in the past when Britannia ruled the waves and gunboat diplomacy was in vogue. Boysie had last seen those photographs at Special Security headquarters. Somehow they were out of place here in the mews flat in which the Chief lived out his retirement. So were the three telephones the old boy sported on his desk. One was a scrambler. The Chief still had contact with power.

"Yes, bleedin' clever idea," Boysie replied without much enthusiasm.

"I don't know about that, Chief. It should bring in a few new pence, though."

"Way of the bloody world," puffed the Chief. "Everything changin', even the old adages. Take care of the new pounds and the new pence will take care of themselves. Damn politicians. Too much arse and no balls. Always said it would come to this. Need Navy men at the top instead of schoolgirl politicians. Never trust a bloody politician, Mostyn."

"No, Chief."

"Have another snort? All this claptrap about freedom. You have to control people properly. Keep 'em under. Discipline. Obedience. People got to know their place. Society's gone queer and we've got to get back to basics."

The Chief poured with a quavering hand and then they got down to what Mostyn called "the incidental routine legal matters". Boysie signed a number of documents most of which were unread. Three large brandies with Mostyn and several snorts of champagne at the Chief's had done their work.

Finally, with all things completed and a cheque for five hundred pounds handed to Boysie for grooming, they all grinned stupidly.

"I think," said Mostyn, "that you'd better come on down and inspect the office."

The office was in Knightsbridge but did not live up to Boysie's expectations. There was a large reception, a roomy office for the secretary, and his own den, yet the furnishings were mundane, without the expected flair. He voiced a protest to Mostyn.

"Can't have everything at once, old son. Got to provide you with three dollies to double as secretaries, receptionists and ground hostesses. Going to cost a pretty penny. Uniforms as well. Not cheap, sport, not cheap."

"Going to look a bit out of place against this tatty background," observed Boysie.

"Up to you, son. Set 'em to work. Amazing what the right girls will do if you instil enough loyalty into them. Lick of paint here and there. Boyfriends in the trade. Flash furnishings at cheap rates. You'll see. There'll be an office float, of course. We'll be generous."

Their advertisement appeared in the *Standard* on the following evening:

Three exceptionally well-polished girls required to do secretarial and other duties. Work will bring them into close contact with the general public. Must have bright swinging personalities and ability to deal with horrific situations. Great prospects including dress allowance and travel.

"Dress allowance sounds better than 'uniform'," said Mostyn.

"What about 'travel'?" asked Boysie.

"Ah." Mostyn tapped the side of his nose with a forefinger. "They'll be going to Gatwick and Heathrow, places like that. That's travelling, isn't it?"

It seemed that many young women were in need of employment. The office was flooded with calls and, by the following morning, when they got around to interviewing the applicants, the place began to resemble open night in the harem.

The ladies came in great variety. Reception blossomed with maxis, minis, pant suits, chain belts, beads, fright wigs, the weird and the wonderful. Breasts peeped bare from lattice work and thighs strained leaping from high-hitched hems. Black, white, coffee, yellow, strained grey: the whole range of skin tones were on show, together with a spectrum of scents, from Patou's *Joy* to natural unwashed armpit and worse.

Boysie regarded the herd with hungry eyes.

"We are not here, old lad, to find you a soul bird but to choose three choice morsels who will work hard and make the office a shade easier to bear." Mostyn had now adopted a manner which was totally authoritarian, his voice flowing on a stream of golden syrup sprinkled with sand.

In the process of weeding the ewes from nannies, during the first interviews, Mostyn had one trick question: "How long were you in your last job?" If the applicant answered in figures amounting to more than three weeks he would smile his dangerous smile and hiss, "Prove it."

The dolly ladies came and the dolly ladies went.

At last they were left with the final trio, splendid specimens, each the proud possessor of almost identical statistics around 36–24–35.

Miss Eutropia Evesham-Bonnard stood five feet eleven inches in her bare feet, had skin the colour and texture of the proverbial creamed peaches, blonde hair, shoulder length and as unruly as silk in a wind tunnel.

"Eutropia," mused Boysie. "Unusual name."

"She was a saint." Miss Evesham-Bonnard's voice came with a thousand strings and the throaty cry of profound sensuality. It lit the day for both men. "A saint," she repeated. "Saint Eutropia, virgin and martyr."

"A paradox," said Mostyn.

Miss Lollo Merry N'Boffs was an inch shorter than Eutropia. Her skin was a glistening shade of milk chocolate. Lollo Merry came from Ghana and her laugh held the bubbling promise of all things bright and feminine.

Miss Jenny Ho Ching Ye was tall for a Chinese girl. She came from Hong Kong and carried herself with the careless assurance of youth. Her hair was jet, her colour golden and to look into her eyes was to see through one hundred fathoms of warmth.

Mostyn explained the operations of Air Apparent and gave the girls a brief outline of their duties. He introduced Boysie and turned to a more difficult aspect.

"I'm sure you'll all agree to my next suggestion. Here at Air Apparent we look for individuality, but we like the customer to feel that while he is travelling with us he is part of the organisation."

You had to admit it, Mostyn's guile was unbeatable. "You must be easily identifiable, so, during working hours I would like each of you to assume a new identity, a new name. Lollo Merry will be known as Aida; Jenny as Alma; and Eutropia as Ada."

"As long as you pronounce it *ardour*," pouted the newly-christened Ada.

Mostyn had the grace to smile.

"You will also wear the Air Apparent hostess uniform. If you go straight away to the address which I shall give to Ada, Mister Gotlieb, who has designed the uniform for us, will measure you and see that your every want is supplied. Report here for duty on Monday at ten."

"Lashing it around with specially designed uniforms, aren't we?" Boysie looked quizzically at Mostyn once the girls had departed. Mostyn flapped a hand for silence and went on dialling, his index finger prodding at the telephone like a small urchin on a private delousing quest. Eventually he got through and spoke. "Solly? . . . Good. Jimmy Mostyn here, the girls are on their way. They're all around the six foot mark like you said, so you shouldn't have any trouble. Just don't forget what I said, don't maul the merchandise . . . Right . . . Fine Solly . . . No, I promise you'll have no more trouble after this . . . Good . . . Goodbye." He looked up at Boysie, grinning. "Old mate, Solly Gotlieb, got landed with a load of hot material, red gaberdine. Been very worried about it until I showed him the way to the paths of righteousness."

"You're a proper bastard, aren't you?"

"Absolute, Boysie. Gold-plated. Well I'm off to Lisbon and then sunny black Africa. Mind the store and look after the girls. You shouldn't have any trouble with Old Portnoy's complaint now. I'll be in touch." With a light snarl Mostyn was gone: a magician's exit.

Boysie, now left with the best part of a week to set himself up as a man about Air Apparent, went out into the world of Mr Fish and Pierre Cardin, Liberty, Simpsons and every trendy male boutique in town. New clothes made him feel brighter and sharper than he had done for the months of his lazing. A fresh hair style appeared to inject liberal supplies of hormones into his flagging body.

On Monday morning, making his first official appearance at the office, Boysie admitted, even to himself, that he had begun to feel respectably horny.

The condition was advanced with speed when he set eyes on the three girls identically clad in warm scarlet micro dresses: tunics with short sleeves, roll collars and set off with wide buckle belts. Each had her name embroidered on the left breast in gold. Together they sent Boysie's imagination boggling down the slopes of permissiveness. The girls lost their poise momentarily as they crowded into Boysie's office chattering about how much they liked their uniforms.

"We have pants to wear with the tunics while doing hostess duties. Beautiful flared bottoms," enthused Aida.

"And we've all bought matching knickers," drawled Ada.

"Scarlet Sin they are called," commented Alma.

"Yes." Boysie felt suddenly rather parental. He leaned forward, hands on the desk. "Well, here we all are. There isn't really any specific work to do as yet, but. . . ."

"Oh, isn't there?" Mostyn stood in the doorway. "No work and all play makes Jack a very dull boy." He advanced towards the desk nodding at the girls. "And Jill an extremely dull girl. We are now operational. The first flight goes out from Gatwick at twenty-three hundred hours on the twentieth of the month. You have ten days to fill it." Briefcase onto the desk and snapped open revealing bundles of green ticket forms. "The advertisement goes in tonight's *Standard* and the charter is with Excelsior Airways. All passengers will automatically become members of the Johannesburg Society of Architectural Admiration. Backdated six months. Onward and upward, my dear children."

3

He was a tall very thin man of about fifty. The few strands of preserved hair were slicked close onto his scalp giving the effect of hard dark ridges cut into the tight pink skin.

He was not a tidy man: his suit needed cleaning and the tie, which had seen better times, was carelessly knotted. It was cold in the office and the cold always made his nose run. He presumed this had something to do with his affliction. The thin man had a cleft palate.

The gas fire also had an affliction: two broken bars. It popped uneasily and did not function with maximum efficiency. The thin man looked at it as a nervous person will stare at dangerous creeping insects at the zoo. He then turned his gaze in a melancholy manner to the desk burgeoned with papers. He often told people that the office was inadequate. Just the two small rooms above the undertaker's shop (a window cleaned twice weekly; a black curtained backdrop and one single vase of plastic flowers). You entered straight from the street and up the steep uncarpeted stairs that were so difficult for Pesterlicker's chair.

Pesterlicker was not in this morning so they did not have the drama with the chair. But the size of the office was always a drama.

Papers and files covered most of the room, cascading from desk to chair to floor, then rising onto the makeshift shelves, rough wooden boards bracketed onto the wall. There was a single window, set in a wooden peeling white frame, through which one gained an inspiring view of a high brick wall.

Somewhere from beneath the papers a telephone began to ring.

He rummaged and finally drew the instrument from the sea of typescript and forms, its umbilical cord snaking out from between a file, marked JDF PERSONAL, and a thick batch of newspaper cuttings stapled together. The top cutting bore the headline *Haulage Contractor Denies Unsafe Vehicles Charge*.

"Echo," he said into the telephone receiver, only, because of his cleft palate, it came out as "Eh-oh."

"Little Sir," said the voice at the other end of the line. It was a male voice, clear and tinged with the gravel of London.

"Ood mornin' Itul Hir."

"Mornin' Echo, I think we're on to the right one. It's all workin'. They call themselves Air Apparent. Their front man's an ex-security bloke called Oakes—they've arranged a charter for the twentieth with Excelsior."

"Hounds right. I hink it's hime ouee hut Ma-ha Hari on hoo it."

"Shall I give you the details then?"

"Nyes hlease."

The man with the cleft palate listened for three minutes, occasionally noting a point in pencil on the back of a telephone directory that he pulled from among the litter on the floor.

When Little Sir had finished, Echo put down the telephone, delved among the papers and found the main body of the instrument. He pushed down the receiver rests and began to dial carefully.

Miss Snowflake Brightwater responded to the melodic tone of her telephone with instant happiness. She ran naked from the brass fourposter draped in billowing light blue hangings. The telephone was an original from around 1910: a beautiful stand model in brass and ebony, hence the pleasing tone of the bell.

Early in her teens, Snowflake Brightwater had decided to fill her life and surroundings only with the most decorative and feminine objects. Feminity, and the woman's rôle of serving the male to make him happy, was her calling. In this she was a paradox. She despised the tough striding mini-skirted dollies jackbooting it through offices or exploding with dirty laughter and back slapping on equal terms with men. Yet Snowflake had to work in order to fill her life with femininity. She preferred work out of the normal public domain. Work, she held, was not a thing to be flaunted by a woman. It made her too much a man's equal: the last thing she wanted. The equality of the sexes being abhorrent to her, Snowflake considered that those foolish young women who fought for the right were ninnies of the highest order. All that was precious to Snowflake lay in the duty of serving her masters: known and unknown.

"Hallo." She breathed a small warm zephyr into the telephone's mouthpiece. From where she stood she could view her body in the long gilt-framed mirror on the opposite wall. The mirror was flanked by large poster portraits: Ché Guevara; Francis Albert Sinatra; John Lennon and Edward Heath. Snowflake Brightwater was politically confused.

The voice at the far end of the telephone caused her to stiffen and cease admiring her reflection. She gave her whole attention to the caller, nodding from time to time and saying "Yes, Mister Frobisher . . . No, Mister Frobisher . . . Then there's no real hurry, Mister Frobisher? . . . I see, Mr Frobisher . . . The night of the twentieth or after . . . I'll keep in touch, Mister Frobisher. Yes, Mister Frobisher."

Slowly she replaced the receiver onto the outstretched arms of the large brass curved rest. She turned and looked into the mirror again.

Oh brother, Miss Snowflake Brightwater was so gorgeous. From the top of her long auburn hair down the many soft sliding curves and swirls of her golden shape to the pink toes she was a zinger.

Oh Miss Brightwater, she thought, you really have all the things men want from a young well-mannered lady of twenty-eight summers and now it is time to climb into those pretty clothes and go out into the world to set men's blood on fire. You also have work to do. Not the clickity-clack, tring-tring work of the offices, nor the tense restraint of the creative world. For you it is time to begin the secret life: to move on tippy tits through the seductive and luring areas.

Nobody, lovely Miss Snowflake Brightwater, is more suited to do that. With a jerk of her breasts she was off, running with light steps towards the bedroom.

While she had listened to the telephone call, Snowflake had doodled on the scratchpad next to the instrument. One particular doodle ran in bold letters across the page. OAKES, it read.

Far away, from the bathroom with its elegant jars of salts and scents, came Snowflake Brightwater's voice. She sang of places far across the world, and the beauty of her voice nearly made her swoon.

Boysie doodled and hummed as he was doodling. "Fly me to the moon," he hummed. The doodling was being perpetrated on a BOAC timetable. He completed words from the capital letters of BOAC so that it read Boysie Oakes Airline Consortium.

He held the pamphlet at arm's length and studied the effect. It looked great.

In reception and the outer office everything was happening and the girls worked like things demented.

At first, Boysie had doubted that the small ad in the *Standard* would do the trick. It simply said:

YOU WANT, or have, to get to South Africa quickly and cheaply. Luxury flight. Would you believe £69 single fare? Limited offer. Telephone.

There followed the office telephone number. It began to ring within half an hour of the first edition and continued to ring at regular intervals. Five days later, with the ad appearing each day, they had already booked one hundred and twelve seats, taken the money, and parted with the tickets.

Boysie had little to do but check the cash and cart it to the bank. Ada, Alma and Aida chirped around in their red dresses, swirling, bending to reveal the little scarlet nylon bottoms, and ministering to most of Boysie's whims. They were as excited as Boysie to watch the tickets go. More, they were becoming a tiny community. Alma turned out to be a splendid cook. On one evening they had all gone back to her apartment where she had produced a magnificent sweet and sour pork with the speed it takes most girls to open a tin of beans.

The dark Aida also had hidden talents. On the third morning of the inauguration of Air Apparent she had suddenly produced a pen and ink portrait of Boysie which caught his mood and manner exactly. Without thinking, Boysie had gone straight down the road to Harrods to have it framed. Nobody was surprised to hear that Aida had once been an art student. She was immediately commissioned to do some paintings for the office.

Ada was not to be left out. On the previous evening she had invited everybody home for a snack. Mummy and Daddy were out for the evening. Home, they discovered, was practically a baronial hall outside Richmond, and the snack (cold turkey, ham, veal and ham pie, chicken, lobster, and a choice of four wines) was served by a doting, if aged, butler called Fisher.

After the meal Ada asked if anybody ever did any shooting.

"Game or people?" Boysie responded.

"Well in this case, target actually. Daddy and my brother Toby have a pistol range in the cellar if anyone wants a go. Good fun actually."

The others twittered and said they would at least watch and they were sure Boysie was terribly good.

Boysie's stomach went heavy as they tramped down wide stone steps into the cellar. It was a perfect little range, well lit and with four weapons lying on the bench firing position. Boysie flicked his eyes over them with professional interest. Two were .22 target automatics: a Standard Olympic with barrel weights and a High Standard Duramatic. He mentally crossed off both of them. They were purely cardboard target stoppers, cumbersome to carry. At the far end was a chichi, much engraved, .38 Llama VIII. That would do at a pinch but he mistrusted all the swirled engraving. Daddy did not take his pistols seriously. Or did he? Next to the Llama was a .38 Diamondback revolver. Neat, compact. Automatically Boysie went straight to the revolver and weighed it in his hand. It felt right. A long time since he had held anything like this. Memory flooded back with the feel of the gun as he realised the Diamondback was identical to the Python except that it was built to the Police Positive Special size frame.

Once, he had used a Python. He could see the man called Madrigal and feel the revolver kick against his glove. Madrigal lifted from his feet by the impact. A girl running and the Python jerking again. Once. The girl pushed against the wall and sliding down. Blood.

Boysie looked at the gun in his hand and felt disgust.

"Come on, Oaksie, show us." Ada stood at his left holding the Duramatic. She was pushing a box of shells towards him. Down range the little cardboard targets waited neat and clean. Boysie grinned and nodded, swung out the cylinder and began to slide the six shells into place.

"I have first go?" Raised eyebrows towards Ada.

"Go ahead, Oaksie, I'm not very good at it actually."

To be a good pistol man you need daily practice. If you cannot use your weapon live each day you should at least do a dry shoot. In any case there should only be one weapon for one man. The pistol, in the hand of an expert, is nothing more than an extension of the arm: a lethal part of the hand.

The weight of the revolver felt very near to his old requirements, but Boysie knew it was all old dead stuff. He had not shot live for almost eighteen months.

Without thought his body took up his natural firing position, the most comfortable for his personal tastes. Feet apart, body well balanced, side on to the target. He gripped the revolver high on the butt, head steady and eyes focused still and unblinking at the target. Then, fast, gun up, right arm rigid, left hand clutching right. Sights on. Squeeze.

The noise of one shot in the relatively confined space of the cellar was deafening. Squeeze again. The second shot exploded on the ferocious tail of noise trailed by the first. The girls clapped their hands over their ears. He felt his nostrils flare at the old scent. The cordite. Alma's face registered fear. Boysie remained cold, features set as he squeezed again and again until all six shots had gone. Even then he stood motionless, still squared up with the target, for at least the count of ten, before automatically lowering the gun, swinging the cylinder and emptying the spent cases onto the bench. One rolled off and made a long metallic ringing sound, sharp in contrast to the dull ring in their ears.

Ada looked at him strangely. "You've done it before, haven't you? You've done it a lot?"

Boysie shook the mood from him. "Used to. It was my hobby at one time." He tried to grin but his face felt frozen.

Ada reeled in the target. It was not brilliant by his former standards. A one-and-a-half inch group. Central. Better than most people. For a halved second his mind reacted as it had once been trained: not good enough; getting slack and flabby; an hour a day on the range and fifteen minutes dry shooting at home every day; pulling to the right; bad habit. Then he washed it away.

Boysie did not shoot again. The girls had a bang with the Duramatic which did not make so much noise, then they all trouped upstairs to watch the wonders of coloured television and finally to be ferried home in the Bentley.

Boysie sat there still grinning at his doodled joke of Boysie Oakes Airline Consortium. There was a tap on the door and Ada came in. Ada's entrances were things of great moment. She had a more subtle approach than those who throw open doors to make their entrances in the manner dramatic. Ada's technique was to open the door about half way and wiggle through. It was like a dance step: feet and legs, twist of the hips, whole body, then a further twist of the hips which brought her onto the inside of the door.

Boysie enjoyed watching those entrances, especially when she was smiling. She smiled now.

"One hundred and fifty," said Ada.

"Tickets?" Boysie put down the BOAC schedule.

Ada nodded confirmation. "If it goes on like this we'll be home and dried in a couple of days."

"Going like free tea at a Civil Servants' outing. Well done."

"Well done indeed. I've just checked the figures." The ubiquitous Mostyn stood in the doorway. He narrowed his eyes as if squinting through sunlight. "Good God, Boysie, a fancy dress ball?"

Boysie pretended not to notice. He had taken to wearing some of his new gear in the office. The blue velvet flared trousers. Blue silk shirt, puffed sleeves, neckerchief and long bold waistcoat struck him as being exceptionally swinging. It made him look younger as well, what with his hair now trained down in the front of his ears and carefully lacquered. "New image."

"New image my untainted arse." Mostyn turned to Ada. "Scoot." He nodded in the direction of the door. Ada scooted and Mostyn advanced towards the desk, taking up a sitting position and staring with undisguised revulsion at Boysie's shoes which were buckled and in a shade of smoked Corsican. "If the Chief could only see you now."

"Well, he's not likely to see me."

"Oakes gone bloody poofy. I can hear him. Damn nancy boy, tarted up like a prize nympho."

"You want this to be a swinging concern, then you'll have to accept it."

"Don't be damn silly, Boysie. We're in the airline business not dress designing. I want you in here clad like a swinging businessman."

"My garb is not your concern."

"It's very much my concern. This company pays for your gear. I hope to heaven you've got a decent dark suit."

"Why?"

"Because you're going to need it, lad. You'll be out there looking smart and natty in a conventional dark suit on the night of the twentieth."

"The night of the twentieth?"

"Part of your duties include the supervising of passengers to Gatwick and making sure that they all get safely on board Excelsior's Flight 319, lad. You can't do that prancing around in teenage playsuits. We leave that sort of thing to the girls."

Boysie had not yet assimilated the fact that his physical

48

presence would be required in the boarding operation. "What about you?" he asked coldly.

Mostyn smirked. "I shall be in black Africa, son, making certain that all goes well at that end."

"Well out of the way. All right, what am I supposed to do?"

Mostyn made himself more comfortable on the corner of the desk and began to talk. Boysie grew increasingly unhappy.

"The coach driver has his instructions," Mostyn said towards the end of his monologue. "You have no problems as long as you keep to the schedule."

Boysie lifted his melancholy face and mouthed a well-known obscenity.

4

On the morning of the twentieth, Boysie Oakes, dressed in conventional clerical grey and sporting a pink floral tie, strolled down to Harrods. He found the right department, selected his purchase, bought it and carefully carried it back to the office, smuggling it in and hiding the parcel in one of his desk drawers, which he locked.

Early on the evening of the twentieth, Miss Snowflake Brightwater began to prepare for work. After observation and attentive consideration, she had decided that tonight was the night for action. Tonight she had to be a temptress of considerable finesse.

She bathed in fragrant water, powdered her skin with the tenderness of a skilled nurse treating third degree burns, and treated her face with the care Michelangelo must have lavished upon the Sistine Chapel. She then exercised, as she did each morning and evening, marvelling at the suppleness of her limbs.

At last, to the accompaniment of Chopin's Etude in C Minor, Op. 10 No. 12 (she thought the *Revolutionary* stirring for the blood and painfully romantic), Miss Snowflake Brightwater began to dress.

At eight thirty that evening the three girls met Boysie at the office. It was the witching hour, the moment of truth when Boysie had to explain the inner workings of the operation and instruct the girls in the fine art of picking up a large number of passengers from central London and spiriting them to Gatwick Airport.

At first, Boysie regarded this part of the business as a

mere incidental. It was only when Mostyn explained the mechanics that he perceived it was as complicated as a game of snakes and ladders: with real snakes and rubber ladders.

At eleven o'clock that evening almost two hundred men, women and children, plus their baggage, were scheduled to embark on Excelsior's Flight E 319. But, until they checked in at Excelsior's counter in the main concourse at Gatwick Airport, they were the sole responsibility of Air Apparent. This fact made Boysie Oakes a proven and committed blunderer of exacting proportions, their sole guide, confessor and friend.

There was also the problem of gathering together up to two hundred persons and their luggage. Such a group is inclined to take up considerable space, but Mostyn, in his inimitable manner, had thought of a way round this.

First, when issuing tickets the Air Apparent girls were instructed to enquire whether the passengers would make their own way to Gatwick or travel on the official Air Apparent transport. This analysis showed that almost half of the passengers required the company's help. Bearing in mind the fact that they had to look like a regular airline company and act efficiently, Mostyn had made the arrangements. It was, however, up to Boysie and the girls to do the trick. To this end Boysie explained the procedure and sheepishly produced the purchase he had made that morning at Harrods.

The girls applauded with natural glee. Boysie had brought a black, shining-peaked uniform cap.

It is a strange psychological fact that, in a public place, one male dressed in a perfectly normal suit but wearing a uniform cap can create an aura of authority. Wearing that cap and given the necessary confidence, Boysie could have walked on to the Brighton Belle and persuaded the entire travelling population that they were actually being transported to Bournemouth. A peaked cap among uncertain voyagers is a magic hat.

Mostyn was a man expertly conversant with the art of producing instant authority. The cap had been his idea.

He was also responsible for the venue. If you had to manoeuvre a large crowd of anxious people festooned with grips, suitcases, hatboxes and long parcels which seemed to have a life of their own, you marshalled them among others of their ilk. Mostyn could easily have chosen Waterloo Railway Station. In fact he opted for Victoria Coach Station.

It was logical enough, the passengers were to be transported by coach. The true problem lay in the fact that Air Apparent had no means of providing a coach service directly from the Station and certainly no possible authority for setting up a recognised office within the station's confines.

But Mostyn was a fixer, a promulgator. He gave the orders and set the thing up. He had provided that each ticket gave details of the coach departure time from Victoria Terminal. He organised a pair of sixty-eight seater coaches, and had already bribed the drivers from the hire firm to have the vehicles in position along Buckingham Palace Road at nine thirty. Mostyn was not troubled with the fact that it was illegal to load coaches in Buckingham Palace Road, nor was he particularly worried about how Boysie and the girls would sort out and guide the passengers from the coach station round the corner to the coaches. As far as Mostyn was concerned, Buckingham Palace Road was near to the coach station and the passengers would assemble themselves in the station. Boysie's job, he considered, was mere child's play.

The girls re-checked the booking schedules. Ninety-six people had elected to be transported from Victoria to Gatwick.

At exactly nine fifteen, the three girls, bright in their scarlet tunics and flared pants, with Boysie, resplendent in peaked cap, disembarked from a cab outside the coach station's main entrance.

It was a mild night, but no stars ever shine for Victoria Coach Station, which is London's limbo: a place for those inescapably in transit. There is a sadness about the drab place. The Englishman's natural modes of transport are the automobile and the railway train. Railway stations indeed are places of high drama and adventure. Not so coach stations.

In the United States the coach depot is more natural. There is a sense of exploration about "Coach boarding at gate five is the coach for Cheyenne, Laramie, Medicine Bow, Walcott, Rawlins, Rock Spring, Green River and Ogden." Victoria Coach Station cannot match that; not even with "The coach for Leeds will be leaving an hour late."

"Okay girls." Boysie looked at his watch. "Cover the entrances. Eyes down for baggage with Air Apparent stickers and filter 'em off round the corner. Aida will come in with me on the dot of twenty past."

In the next five minutes the girls collected a dozen up-up-and-away customers heading towards the main entrances. They were hustled round the corner to the appointed pick-up zone. Then, with Ada and Alma still circling the main doors, Boysie and Aida made their entrance.

The interior of Victoria Coach Station somewhat resembles a vast garage: a large bleak rectangle with depressing girders supporting the roofing. A wide paved area, forming three sides of a small rectangle, is allotted for departing and arriving passengers who anxiously scan timetables, constantly harass coach company officials, and are moved in small groups by sporadic outbursts from an elemental loudspeaker system.

The paved area was crushed full of people and their baggage. Among them, Boysie knew, would be eighty or so folk already in the mentally suspended state that attacks a herd grouped together for a long, and relatively un-comfortable, aeroplane journey.

As there was no possible reason for this small segment of society being at Victoria Coach Station when they wanted to get onto an aircraft at Gatwick, Boysie's job was to get them out: fast and without official interference.

With Aida at his heels, Boysie began his progress, from one corner of the paved area, heading towards the Bucking-ham Palace Road Exit which lay at the far end. As he moved through the crowd, Boysie chanted loudly. "Air

Apparent Flight E 319. Passengers follow me please. Air Apparent Flight E 319 . . ."

A recognisable look of hope flooded onto numerous faces as they recognised, in Boysie, a mentor to free them from the discomfort of waiting in this drear place. They began to follow.

"Air Apparent Flight E 319 . . ."

"I have all this baggage. What am I to do with my baggage?" A skinny lady in a coney coat blocked Boysie's path, snapping like a worried poodle. The conies looked as though they had been massacred during a famine.

The customer, thought Boysie, is always right. "If you have our labels on the articles just leave them there, madam. Like Zorro I shall return."

There were three other incidents concerning baggage which could not be manhandled by its owners. A fair-sized crowd began to build up behind Boysie: Aida bringing up the rear, whipping in stragglers.

Boysie did not dislike crowds, for they were groups in which one could hide. But here, with the gaggle pressing in on his back and the rising clack of chatter, an edge of panic began to stir: a nervy pressure starting to brew.

"Air Apparent Flight E 319 follow . . ." Boysie's voice continued the exhortation, punctuated now by the responses of those who followed.

"Is this where we get on the aeroplane, Mum?"

"Shut up and hang on to my coat. If you get lost your father'll belt you."

"Disgraceful paying all this money to be treated like this."

An aged gentleman, clutching a lethal walking stick and a bulging carrier bag, pushed through the throng and began to jerk at Boysie's sleeve. It was a temporary setback.

"All right for Sheffield?" shouted the old man.

"Air Apparent Flight E 319 . . ." bawled Boysie, doing his best to push on and ignore all distractions.

"Will that get me to Sheffield?" screeched the aged one.

"Not unless you want to go via the Gold Coast," hissed Boysie.

A small stout woman with tinted glasses and a pull-on

hat the colour of dried sheep's dung appeared at the old man's elbow waving a ticket. "Leeds?" she cawed. "Do we follow you for Leeds?"

Boysie's cool became tepid. He stopped. Several of the following crowd were involved in minor bumper to bumper shunting operations.

"Leeds," said Boysie, his voice quavering a little loudly, "is over there." Pointing far into the cavern of the station. "And Sheffield," rising to a shriek, "is next to Leeds."

The couple nodded enthusiastically and departed never to be seen again.

"Air Apparent Flight E 319. Passengers follow . . ." Boysie glanced behind him at the growing human snake.

"'Ang on a minute. What you think you're up to? Incitin' a bloody riot?"

Boysie's forward movement was blocked by an official looking man with warts, a cap similar to the one Boysie wore, and a long black raincoat.

Boysie gave a sick smile. "Sorry mate. There's been a bit of a cock up. People told to report here by mistake."

"'Ave to report it." Warty produced a notebook and pencil, which he licked, displaying an ugly coloured tongue. "We can't 'ave cock ups in the coach station, it's upsetting to the regular passengers. As Duty Inspector I'll . . ."

"Be all out in a minute." Boysie edged forward. "Tell you what. You phone the gaffer, it's all his fault, brother. I'm only obeying orders. Tool of the capitalist pigs, that's what I am. Phone him. Three-severn-oh, one-nine-two-nine." The numbers had come easily into his head as he lurched off still chanting.

The Duty Inspector scratched his head, made as if to speak, then changed his mind and, with the air of one who has little opportunity of exercising his small authority, began to write in the notebook. As Boysie and the phalanx of passengers moved away, the Duty Inspector stopped writing, looked after them and again scratched his head with the bewildered determination of defeat.

The coaches arrived dead on time and the girls set about getting their passengers on board with as much speed as possible while Boysie, labouring heavily by this time, dashed to and fro collecting the heavy baggage which had been left inside the station.

By nine forty they looked ready to go. Boysie was on the step of the lead coach when Ada ran up, white-faced.

"We've got three too many." She looked genuinely concerned.

"We can't have. How do you know?"

"Alma and I have been counting heads and unless we've got a trio of two-headed freaks we're carrying ninety-nine not ninety-six."

"Check the tickets," ordered Boysie, cavalier to the last.

"Can't wait 'ere any longer," interrupted the driver of the lead coach.

"We'll have to."

"Well, we can't."

"Why not? Give me two good reasons."

The driver looked at him with pity. "First, we shouldn't be here at all. Second, there's the Public Bleedin' Service Vehicles: Conduct of bleeding Drivers, Conductors and bleedin' Passengers Regulations, 1936. Section bleedin' seven, para (b) A-driver-shall-not-cause-the-vehicle-to-remain-stationary-on-a-road-longer-than-is-reasonably-necessary-to-pick-up-or-set-down-passengers-except-at-a-stand-or-place-where-such-vehicles-are-permitted-to-stop-for-a-longer-time-than-is-necessary-for-that-purpose. That's by the bleedin' book."

Happily, by the time the driver had finished reciting regulations, the stowaways had been discovered: a trio of little elderly ladies under the misapprehension that they were on the coach for Middleton-in-Teesdale.

"Stay flexible, keep moving and let it all hang out." Boysie murmured to himself. The brace of coaches pulled away.

On the far side of the street a black, polished Daimler stood at rest. In the rear, comfortable and well-fed, sat a man called Suffix. He was tall with a face full of dubious character: as though his features had regularly been altered with the help of fists, bottles and the sun. His clothing looked casual until you scrutinised and the art of a skilful

56

tailor was revealed: a dark blue denim battledress and matching shirt. Around the neck a silk kerchief and, hanging from a silver chain, a small locket. The locket was executed in silver and carried on its smooth front the raised device of a cobra spitting fire.

Suffix removed the cigarette holder from his lips and addressed his companion, a much older man. "You were right. Quite right. It is amusing to observe humans going to so much trouble in order to perform a simple operation. That's what I find fascinating about Africa. I think we should see them off."

His companion nodded. "Oakes always had a streak of the bizarre. But watch him. Have care."

The Daimler moved away in the wake of the coaches.

From the viewing windows in the gallery of the main concourse at Gatwick you can look out across the parking area to the taxiways and seven thousand feet of runway two seven slicing across rich Surrey countryside.

At night it was a carpet of lanes lit by blue and white grounded stars, backed by the group music of jets.

The chaos of the pick-up at the coach station had quickly subsided once they got under way. There was only minor confusion on arrival at the airport. Within twenty minutes Excelsior had taken over and the responsibility had passed from Boysie's hands.

He sent the girls up to one of the cafeterias to get coffee and sandwiches while he went to watch the departure, leaving the magic cap in Ada's safe keeping. Only some major disaster, like the aircraft being turned back, would return that unruly load of travellers into Boysie's lap.

He could see Excelsior's big Boeing trundling away towards the threshold, its identification lights blinking metronomically.

Slowly the aircraft began to roll, becoming indistinguishable among the pinpoint lights and darkness: then the flashing lights rising. Flight E 319 was on its way. Boysie was conscious of others standing near and peering across the airfield. He breathed out a sigh which was a mental punctuation to his thoughts, a never again determination. Many times previously, Boysie had made up his mind to refuse Mostyn. But this was it. The trapesing around with platoons of people, the ridiculous business at Victoria, humping baggage. Never again.

Locked within this thought as he turned, Boysie saw the girl too late. They collided and he had to leap, with outstretched arms, to stop her falling badly against the plate glass windows.

"I'm terribly sorry."

"Oh. Oh dear."

"You all right?"

"Oh. It was my fault. I wasn't looking."

She was as light as air: fragile. Boysie felt it so strongly that he carried on holding her shoulders to prevent the further tragedy of her body crumbling away.

Her face was shaded by a large floppy black hat which hindered him from seeing even a wisp of hair. Yet the eyes were enough. Large brown eyes with lashes that curved upwards towards slim pencilled brows. Eyes which invited even when tear-stained as they were at this moment.

The remainder of the face was equally inviting. Wide, well-proportioned lips, high cheekbones, skin without a trace of blemish.

"I'm okay, thanks." A soft throaty voice, touched with melody.

"You certain? You're . . ."

Her hand came up and dabbed at her eyes. The hand was white gloved and held a delicate tiny handkerchief. "I know. It's silly, isn't it. Crying like this. I thought I'd be okay. After all he's only my brother."

"Been seeing him off?"

She nodded quickly, lips moving together. Boysie stepped back. Slim and too good to look at, her body encased in a black velvet pant suit, the jacket full waisted, a leather coat trimmed with fur thrown round her shoulders.

"Can I get you a cup of coffee?"

"Oh, that would be lovely." The face under the hat became gilded with pleasure. "You're so kind."

Boysie guided her to the nearest cafeteria, found a table, seated her and made for the bar.

Ada, Alma and Aida were occupying a table near the bar, engrossed in raucous conversation burnished with coarse laughter. They were dishes, thought Boysie, but, compared to his new found friend, they were as tinned peaches are to the real thing. As he came alongside their table he mouthed, "Make your own way back. I'll see you in the morning."

"Who's your white friend, Mr B?" asked Aida in a low voice.

"Careful, Boysie. That looks very expensive," whispered Alma.

"Stick to your own kind, Oaksie darling, that one'll have your wallet and you won't even get her bra size," growled Ada.

"We're not all sex mad," muttered Boysie, turning away to order a brace of coffees.

She had lighted a cigarette and slung her coat over the back of the chair by the time he returned to the table.

"You really are too kind." The tears had gone and colour returned to her face.

"The least I could do after being so clumsy."

She looked round her. "I hate airports. They have so little taste: in the surroundings, the décor, I mean."

Boysie nodded, exhibiting ageless wisdom. "Built for the passage of human cargo," he observed.

"That's awfully good. Human cargo."

"Well, that's just about it nowadays." Boysie clung on to what seemed an advantage. "We all have to conform to the common denominator. We're all human cargo on the freight lines of life." It did not sound like him at all, but seemed to please the girl.

She sighed. "I know. So depressing. I try not to conform. You look like a non-conformist also."

"One tries."

"I started some years ago. I began with my name. I'm Snowflake Brightwater."

Boysie's instinct was to maintain that he was Golden Sunset III. "I'm Boysie Oakes."

Miss Snowflake Brightwater did not seem all that impressed. "Snowflake Brightwater's my given name of course."

"Given?"

"Yes. I gave it to myself. My conformist name was Harriet Hardy. That was too much." She inhaled on her cigarette and expertly expelled the smoke down her enchanting nose.

"I have my Mercedes Benz motor car outside in the park. When we have finished this doubtful coffee, would you care to drive me back to the city? I feel you are to be trusted."

"Yes, I'd love to drive you back, and yes I can be trusted."

Suddenly Miss Snowflake Brightwater erupted into laughter. "You're super. Most men look for an escape route when I pull the quaint bit on them. They think they're hooked with something totally weird."

"It takes all kinds."

"You didn't even bat an eyelid."

"To be honest I'm thinking of writing a monograph on eyelids I have batted." Boysie drained his paper cup. "Do you really call yourself Snowflake Brightwater?"

"Consistently. Makes paying for things by cheque a bit of a performance, but it's my name and I like it."

"And you have a Mercedes Benz motor car?"

"And a splendid apartment in Eaton Place, but don't let the pound signs show too clearly in your hungry eyes. I've worked for everything I own."

Boysie's mind was not homing onto the idea of riches. He blinked himself back into the present. "I never let pound signs show too readily these days," he said soberly. "You took me back for a minute. I used to live near Eaton Place myself. Just off Chesham Place."

"But no more?"

"Long gone, Snowflake Brightwater, long gone."

She put her elbows on the table, resting her chin in her hands. "What do you do to keep body and soul together? You're not a child of nature. That I can tell by your mode of dress and nice manners."

"The quaint bit's showing again."

"It does from time to time. I live with it, like a second skin. It keeps out those I want to exclude: including thoughts. What do you do?"

"I'm in the airline business." It sounded respectable and was technically true: until he handed his resignation to James George Mostyn, CMG, CBE.

The slim lines that served as eyebrows tilted fractionally upwards. "That rubbish?"

"It puts food on my back and gives me clothes to eat."

She dropped her hands. "Yes, I know. Warms you in summer and keeps you cool in winter. I have similar problems."

Boysie had the sense not to press. He felt that Snowflake Brightwater was a person who only volunteered information of her own sweet accord; certainly never under duress.

She did most of the talking on the way back to town: mainly surface stuff about her childhood. You felt it was genuine enough but it came out flat, unvarnished.

Her father had been a solicitor: small town; south of England; everybody thinking they knew everybody else's business. He had gone into local government and began to imagine he was the PM. Her childhood memories were of that drab security which can only eventually breed discontent in growing youth. The house; school, with regulation uniform: "Grey, Boysie. You know. Grey sacks and grey felt hats, grey ankle socks, grey knickers that scratched. That's the ultimate of English jokes isn't it? God, they'd have had us in grey vests if it wasn't too costly."

Regulations. Keeping up with the Jones's, the Smiths, the ultramarine Browns. Identical televisions, identical pools in the garden, identical ponies; holidays; church on Sunday and more regulations.

In the end she revolted. A perfectly normal breakaway. "I really felt like a trapped animal. Caged. I saw the rest of my life being swallowed up. They already had a couple of nice boys standing in line for me. I was being chained down while the world, on the other side of the hill, ran past faster than sound. So I gave my virginity to a garage hand and quietly stole away."

61

So it was the classic tiptoe down the stairs with the small case, the note, the train and the big city. Her monologue stopped at the big city.

"Does it make sense, Boysie?"

He nodded behind the wheel, the grey ribbon of road being devoured by the singing wheels.

"A lot of sense. You ever go back?"

"Now?"

"Uh-hu."

"Oh yes, now. That's where I'm my most quaint. My mother's the one who really understands. What about you?"

Boysie fired off a couple of well rehearsed salvos of background. The Berkshire village; the downs; war; a lifetime of non-involvement. He went into neither the post-war activities nor the hidden part of youth. It was easy, because he had done it so many times before.

"Do you ever go back?"

"Never." Quick. A door of ten inch steel slamming in the mind, cutting off the truth.

She guided him to the converted house in Eaton Place. He found a parking space and she asked him up for "smoked salmon sandwiches and whatever I've got".

The apartment reflected her quaint disguise. Clean and perfectly kept yet littered with oddments: a huge musical box, little ornaments, bits of china, exquisite but matching nothing, there was even a small stuffed bird in a glass case.

"He looks so sad and tender, don't you think?"

Boysie could not tell if she was sending him up or whether that was an area where the quaintness had taken over from her real self.

She hung up her coat, pulled off her hat and shook out her hair. It was, as Boysie had feared, long, auburn and of a texture which made you wish to bathe in it.

"Food?" Her eyes steady on his.

He shrugged. "Not unless . . ."

"I'm not hungry. But I'm sure you'd like a drink. What is your usual potion?"

"A tincture of brandy, perhaps?"

She smiled, the eyes sparkling. "I have something very

special for you, Boysie Oakes." She bent forward and touched his lips with hers. Miss Snowflake Brightwater tasted good enough to savour at great length. Suddenly she straightened up. Her tone was serious. "Remember. Whatever. I really do like you. Really. Truly." Like a small child. Then the smile again and softly, "The bedroom's through there."

This, thought Boysie, must be the feeling you get when you win the pools.

The bedroom was, naturally, over-decorated; the large brass fourposter looking madly excessive even to Boysie.

"Not in bed yet." She came in behind him carrying a brandy goblet. "Drink that. It will provide the stamina you need. I won't be long." She was out of the room quickly.

You do not argue with the whims of fate. Boysie had learned that many years ago. You took what was offered when it was offered unless you thought there was a chance of a better deal. He sipped the brandy, running his tongue around his mouth.

He took another draught while hanging up his jacket and trousers. It had the smooth bite of age. Another large sip after removing his shirt and socks. This, he considered, was one of the best brandies ever tasted.

Naked, he sipped again and again and felt at peace with the world, greatly taken with Miss Snowflake Brightwater and visibly prepared for any rigours which might follow.

Her sheets were silk soft, the pillow as he had always imagined swansdown should feel. The whole process of lying there and waiting for the door to open was drenched in a self-perpetuating eroticism.

The door slowly opened and Miss Snowflake Brightwater drifted into the room. She wore a long white gown made up from many layers of diaphanous material.

"Comfortable?"

"Gloatingly."

"You feel good?"

"As gold. Gold rampant."

"Good."

Miss Snowflake Brightwater allowed the robe to slide

from her shoulders, revealing slim curves and pink flesh covered only by lavender bra and briefs, characteristically ruffled by bows and lace. Miss Snowflake Brightwater knew how to please and pamper men's small whims.

Boysie felt the warmth of her as she slid in beside him. Thigh to thigh. His lips sought her and her hand moved, unerring as a missile, for him. He felt her touch; her lips engulfing him. Only at the last moment was there a leap of anxiety: a flash of perception. But it was too late, he seemed to experience the sensation of having his brain sucked into Miss Snowflake Brightwater's mouth. Disappearing into the darkness, at the moment of departure, he muttered, "What a lovely way to go."

5

HER HAND WAS on his brow and he had total recall. There was a lot of light. Daylight. He knew about Snowflake Brightwater. He knew she was a beautiful, desirable ethereal lady; that she wore lavender coloured pants; that she had seduced him; that she had conned him.

"You've done for me. You've bloody taken me for the oldest ride. Lured me."

"Shshsh. By the most ancient bait, Boysie. But it may be good yet. Does your head hurt? Can you sit up?"

His head did not hurt and he could sit up quite easily.

It was only when he actually did achieve a sitting position that he realised the room was full of people. He was naked. He could tell that. Miss Snowflake Brightwater was clothed: moulded into a smart skimpy black number.

He blinked and tried to sort things out. The room was not so full as he had first imagined. Apart from Miss Brightwater there were three other people, ranged in a line down the side of the bed. A tall, sad-looking man who seemed in need of repair, and a bald benign negro. Between them, in an invalid chair, sat the top half of a small young man. All three nodded greetings.

"What gives?" asked Boysie, his mind a rubbish bin of possibilities. This could be anything. He had been alert to the past creeping up on him before Air Apparent got its claws into his time and energy. For a short period his guard had dropped. The nerves sang and his stomach performed a tattoo of unpleasant spasms.

"Istah U-Ian Oakes?" asked the tall man.

"You what?"

"He asked if you are Mr Brian Oakes," said the half person in the wheelchair.

"H-h-h-he h-h-h-has an impedi-impediment in h-h-his spee-speech, m-m-m-man," stuttered the coloured egg-head.

"It would be best if I explained." The one in the wheelchair had an unpleasant, nasal voice. "This—" indicating the tall man with the cleft palate—"is Mr Frobisher. I am his associate: Pesterlicker. We are from the Investigation Branch of the Ministry of Transport and Civil Aviation."

Frobisher said something quite unintelligible.

"Quite. We *are* the Investigation Branch. This gentleman," Pesterlicker gestured towards the spade, "is Mr Colefax from the Investigation Branch of the Board of Trade. Is that clear?" The question was menacing.

"Who are you?" Boysie asked Miss Snowflake Brightwater.

"I'm Miss Brightwater."

"We sometimes call her Mata Hari as a jest." It did not sound exactly like that, coming from Frobisher who began to giggle.

"Very comical." There was a shade of relief. This was not Boysie's past giving him trouble. Only the present. Only, he thought. Bloody Mostyn's caught me by the natural privates again.

"You got ID?" Boysie asked flatly.

The trio moved as one: right hands into breast pockets, producing small plastic flip open books which they manoeuvred in front of Boysie's eyes. They looked genuine.

"We have questions to ask," said Pesterlicker.

"By what right?"

"B-b-by th-th-the right that y-y-y-ou're l-lyin' in b-b-bed na-naked and there are th-three of u-us." Colefax pressed his point.

"Four of you," Boysie corrected, looking nastily at Miss Snowflake Brightwater.

"Three of them," she said sweetly. "I do jobs like this for money. I work for them but I don't get involved more than I can help."

"You'll have to be this time." Frobisher had stopped giggling but was still difficult to follow.

"We will see." Miss Snowflake Brightwater played tantalisingly with the hem of her skirt which was hoisted splendidly high.

"You ought to get something done about your speech problem." If it was going to be on the personal level, Boysie reckoned he could play the game as well.

"I huppose ooo hink hat's hunny?" countered Frobisher. "Sh-houldn't w-w-we ge-ge-ge-t on w-w-with th-the b-business?"

"Yes," snarled Pesterlicker. "The business. The business is Mr Oakes. Question one. Are you the Managing Director of a company known as Air Apparent Limited?"

Boysie shrugged. "Yes." The heat was on.

"Are you aware that you have contravened the regulations laid down by the International Air Transport Association, the Board of Trade and the Ministry of Transport and Civil Aviation?"

"No."

"Well, it is our duty to inform you that you have. In fact you have contravened some thirty-eight clauses in these regulations and ignorance of those regulations is no defence in law."

"When did I do it?"

"Over the past few weeks and specifically last night."

"I want to be legally represented."

"Why?"

"I feel I should be represented. If you're going to throw the book at me then I should have a qualified defence."

"Nobody said we were going to throw the book at you." A terrible jumble of words.

Pesterlicker gave Frobisher a look which bade him to shut his deformed vocal exit.

"W-we d-don't w-w-work li-like th-that, ma-ma-man," grinned Colefax.

Pesterlicker sighed. "This is not the middle ages, Mr Oakes. We do not act like the Inquisition or the Star Chamber. I will admit that we do a nice little line in intrigue. But, when we've got something good going for us we are not anxious to louse it up by introducing legions of lawyers."

"You want a cut." All seemed revealed. "Well I can't say yes or no. There are other people involved."

Pesterlicker shook his head. "We were told that you were a person of basic motivations and instincts. They are too basic. We are representatives of Her Majesty's Government and you don't think representatives of Her Majesty's Government would run a protection racket?"

"Is that the sixty-nine dollar question?"

"We know there are other people involved. It is the other people we are after." Pesterlicker allowed what passed for a smile to linger momentarily on his lips.

"They are soliciting your aid, Boysie," whispered Snowflake Brightwater.

Mostyn, thought Boysie. That's who they wanted. At last someone had really caught up with the little, oily-haired, tight-arsed, plum-mouthed, hogwash-piddling, steam-blowing, foot-licking, gut-shaking, nerve-breaking Mostyn.

His mouth split into the friendliest of grins. "Someone else you want?"

Pesterlicker smiled and nodded like a youthful buddah. "Several persons. To that end we are prepared to overlook the charges that could be brought against you in your capacity as Managing Director of Air Apparent. In fact, for a time we are even willing to allow you to continue."

"Ah."

"On the understanding that you report to us and keep your eyes open."

"For what?"

"For anything untoward. Especially concerning the aircraft you charter. But we want everything, no matter how small."

"Done. How do I contact you?" Boysie saw a quick way out. If he got rid of this unfortunate trio he could resign and be away. His share of the present loot would at least get him out of the country for a while.

"You don't contact us." Pesterlicker looked grave. "You do not seem to have grasped one essential fact."

"We are agents."

"Y-y-yea. W-w-we c-come and g-g-go w-w-with st-stealth."

"They're like wraiths. Hush-hush men." Snowflake Brightwater gave Boysie a sympathetic look.

"Oh yes." Boysie jerked his head. "I mean you're just like ghosts, aren't you? Melt into the crowd and all that sort of thing. Once seen immediately forgotten."

The three investigation men nodded. "That's it. You will use Miss Brightwater as a post office. All information will be transmitted through her. You agree to this?"

The prospect brightened. "I agree."

Pesterlicker held up a hand. "Should you fail to provide the required information I must warn you that we can be ruthless."

"Ooee'll hscroo yoo."

"Writs, su-summonses and Hi-hi-hi . . . C-courts."

"You will make your arrangements with Miss Brightwater." Pesterlicker nodded, his companions bowed and they began to make a painful exit.

"Oy," called Boysie, tethered to the bed by his natural modesty.

They turned.

"Don't you think I should know more?"

"No." Pesterlicker spoke quietly. "We work on the need-to-know principle. All you need to know is that we want every piece of information that comes your way."

They left, with Miss Snowflake Brightwater in the rear. "I'll be back," she whispered, closing the door.

Boysie reached for his cigarettes, lit one, reclined on the pillows and pondered. Mostyn had originally recruited him for that dangerous part of his past he had now put behind him. Yet Mostyn was eternally to be associated with evil. Not evil in any abstract sense, but the real and apparent evil which always seemed to be around on a Mostyn-motivated scene. Death, broken bones, gashed bodies, torture, wilful nerve-grating and the dark fantasies of the night were things that came with Mostyn's presence. When Frobisher, Pesterlicker and Colefax spoke of getting another person connected with Air Apparent they could only mean Mostyn. It was a thought more comforting than all the television religious programmes that had ever been.

Miss Snowflake Brightwater returned.

"Nice friends you've got." Boysie blew a mouthful of smoke towards the ceiling.

"Quaint." She came closer.

"What did you put in my drink?"

"I don't know. They gave it to me. It worked at the speed of light, did it not?"

"Did it not," agreed Boysie.

She stood quite close to the bed now. "I'm sorry about all that, truly I am. I have obligations to them. But to prove that I am enamoured of you Boysie, darling, shall we carry on where we left off?"

"Betcha," said Boysie.

"Betcha what?"

"Betcha got black lace pants under that."

"It's the English way of life. As I said last night, dear Boysie, the English joke is knickers; English sex is black lace knickers. It's the Public School system that does it." She raised her hem to pull the dress over her head.

His full name was Colonel Peter Suffix. His London address was Flat 5, Cardigan House, W.1.

The apartment was austere. No carpets or luxury trappings. True, a few books lined one shelf in the main living room, but they were text books, political and military. Suffix sat at a long bare table: a standard issue War Department table from World War Two. He worked with maps and a compass. The telephone rang.

"Suffix." He was a man of few words when it came to telephones.

"Oakes spent the night with Brightwater." The voice at the other end was quiet and sounded young. "They were visited at seven this morning."

"Who?"

"A spade, a guy in a wheelchair and one other."

"Not known?"

"Not to me."

"Follow Oakes. If he goes near the Brightwater again you had better do both of them. Put together, their records

70

are not good. If they're forming a team better to knock them out early."

"Right."

Suffix closed the line and went back to his work.

It was almost noon when Boysie walked into the office. As expected he was greeted by howls and catcalls.

"Her place or yours?" from Alma.

"I don't believe it. Not that one," commented Ada.

"She cook breakfast, Mr B?" asked Aida.

"Would you?" retorted Boysie, glowing as he realised there was a pinch of jealousy in the girls' attitude.

"Anything happened while I've been gone?"

"Not awfully much," said Ada.

"Our precious Flight E 319 had a spot of bother." Aida dropped it with a gleam of her teeth.

The loose sensation in the lower gut. "What's happened?"

"They had to make an emergency landing at Otuka."

"Where's Otuka?" Looking about vainly for a map.

"Capital of Etszika."

"And where the hell's Etszika?"

"Little democratic republic between Gabon and the Congo. West Africa. No sweat. People friendly. I myself once knew a witch doctor from Etszika. Nice man, cured my grandmother's warts." She gave a mock sigh. "Anyway, the trouble's fixed and Flight E 319 is on its way again. All came in on the magic teletype via Excelsior."

"Onward and bloody upward." Boysie leaped towards his office.

The teletype message gave the bare essentials so he called Excelsior. The flight was all right and on its way, having lost an hour. Minor engine fault and worry over fuel. It was all standard practice and they did not sound concerned.

He got down the atlas and looked up the minute square of land that was Etszika. It was difficult to equate the dot that said Otuka with men, women, children and an aircraft. The one bright thought was that the incident gave him something to report: an excuse to see the enchanted Miss Brightwater again and soon.

He called her and she was more than willing to see him that evening. "I shall cook us a meal of vast gastronomic interest and I expect you to wait on me at half past the hour of seven, for eight o'clock. We will drink a little sherry wine first."

She greeted Boysie at the door wearing a claret velvet hostess skirt and white blouse with many ruffles, puffed sleeves and a high neck fastened with a cameo brooch. Her hair was piled on top of her head and looked ravishing.

"Oh, Miss Snowflake Brightwater, I am so glad I found you." Boysie took her in his arms and hugged her. It was a new, safe feeling.

The sherry was light and exquisitely dry (Miss Brightwater seemed to be blessed with the gift of divining Boysie's taste.) The banter was as light as the sherry.

Promptly at eight they moved into the small dining room. The table gleamed with silver and had about it the look of intimacy.

"I have taken much trouble, Boysie, dear." She indicated his chair. "Much more trouble than I would normally take. But you are different."

She left the room, returning a few minutes later bearing a tray on which stood their soup plates and a small tureen.

"Messrs Crosse and Blackwell's famous pea soup," she announced, sweeping the lid from the tureen.

The soup was followed by delicious Plumrose chopped ham with pork and a mixed salad dressed to perfection.

"The dressing is Mr Kraft's Thousand Islands. Piquant, wouldn't you say?"

"It has an edge: an excellent edge for the taste buds."

They completed the banquet with a Findus choc nut mousse. "Such an exciting new flavour," she commented.

"I'll wager the coffee is from Monsieur Nescafé."

"Who else? Gold Blend though."

They both collapsed in giggles over the table. As they sipped coffee, Boysie told her of the emergency landing.

"I shall commit all relevant details to memory; after which I think we should retire early."

She was just opening the bedroom door when the bell rang.

"Two gentlemen for you, Boysie."

"Not again. We went through that routine this morning."

"I know them not." Her hand to her lips.

Boysie put his jacket on again and went into the living room.

They were a pair of well set up young men: neat, carefully dressed and with bright faces.

"Mr Oakes?" asked one.

"Yes."

"Miss Brightwater?"

"Yes."

"I am Paul. This is Charles."

They all nodded and acknowledged the introductions.

"What can I do to help?" Boysie was at ease.

"Just put on your coats and come with us."

"What for?"

"We've come to kill you, but it would make too much noise here," said Charles.

"Must think of other people," said Paul.

6

THE NOISE BEHIND him was Snowflake Brightwater's
breathing. The quick intake of air and the small sighs
through the nostrils. It was the sound of a terrified animal
and served to increase comprehension. The mind said it
was impossible, but Boysie's instinct and heart told him that
it was all too real. The sounds from Snowflake Brightwater
underlined the truth. This was the end game.

Boysie glanced behind him. Snowflake Brightwater's
face was the colour of a dirty grey sky; she held on to a chair
back, leaning forward, in shock.

His mind and vision cleared. Now he could fully dis-
tinguish and identify the two young men. Paul was the
blond, hair trimmed to the nape of the neck; blue eyes; dark
overcoat. Charles wore a navy raincoat; he had brown hair
fashioned like Peter's; slightly more thickset than his
companion.

The genuine articles, thought Boysie. Not crew-cut skin-
heads or bully-boy yobos. They were the kind Mostyn
would pick. He tried to detect the essential emotions behind
their eyes.

"If you wouldn't mind," prompted Paul. "We'd rather
like to get going." He had a hunk of metal in his hand to
reinforce the argument. The hunk of metal looked like a
Walther PPK, but it did not matter about the make. It
was bloody lethal whatever factory it came from.

Boysie raised his arms. "Why?"

"Ours not to reason . . ." began Charles. "Just get your
coats on. I promise it will be easier this way."

A Mostynian remark. These two had to come from
Mostyn. The three stooges with their stutters, impediments

74

and physical imperfections had been real also and Mostyn knew about it. Now it was Mostyn's revenge.

Cut. Stop. Wash the mind. That was easy logic. No proof. Concentrate on dealing with the situation.

"I'll get the coats." Snowflake Brightwater barely audible behind him.

Paul followed her from the room. Charles kept his eyes on Boysie. No flicker. Nerveless. Intelligent robots who had been ordered to kill and would do so to a plan, a programme.

Paul was helping him into his coat.

"There now. All ready?" The soft voice. Queen?

Boysie turned to face Snowflake Brightwater.

"Boysie?" she whispered, her face already cast in the bewildered expression of sudden death.

Boysie stopped and turned his attention to Paul. "How?" he asked simply.

"There is a motor car downstairs. We will get into it and drive to a secluded spot. After that we will shoot you. I promise it'll be quick and merciful."

Mostyn? The three stooges? The past? The past? The past?

It was a dark coloured Mark Ten Jaguar. The man at the wheel was also young and presentable. He nodded in a friendly way as they climbed in. Charles in front. Snowflake and Boysie in the back with Paul sitting sideways on.

Boysie was sweating; he could smell his own sweat; Snowflake Brightwater clung to his hand, encased in her own misery and fear.

He tried to speak but there was difficulty. When the words did come out he experienced a flicker of shame at the nervous quake in his voice.

"I can understand someone wanting to get me, but I don't see why the girl . . .?"

"Schtum," said Paul. "It's easier without the chat. Better for all: that way nobody gets emotionally involved."

Boysie knew the technique. In books and movies there was always the car ride which gave the hero a chance to think, act and escape. In real death it was preferable to do the job on the spot. When you had to cart a mark to some place of execution you did not talk to him. You either did it by conning him into thinking he was being taken to friends, or you told him the truth and hoped that shock would keep him silent until you pulled the trigger. There was a lot about that in the ghastly manual they kept in Whitehall.

He desperately tried to pull his conscious thoughts onto the possibilities of getting clear, but the subconscious kept interrupting. Darkness; non-existence; unknowing. Fear.

They were going east. Stepney? The Docks? It would make sense. A piece of deserted ground. The traffic had begun to thin out and pavements were less occupied. The lighting system was not as good either.

Boysie squeezed Snowflake Brightwater's hand.

She nodded in the darkness, then her profile was suddenly illuminated by a street light: a wash of brightness; her face; then a dimming to darkness.

"Next on the right," Paul quietly told the driver.

"Okay, I know. We've collected something behind. He's running on sidelights, can you see him?"

A pinpoint of hope.

Then, from Paul. "It's only a cab. Probably the driver going home early."

They slowed and took the right turn. A narrow road bordered by brick walls.

"He's coming as well." The driver; a click of urgency in his voice.

"Okay," drawled Paul. "Pull over. Let him pass. Nice and easy."

The driver slowed. Boysie could see his indicator on the dashboard flashing left. He looked to the right and saw the cab pulling level. There was a coloured man at the wheel. He did not even look in their direction. Nor did the four passengers, also coloured.

The driver of the Jaguar began to move forward again as the taxi cleared his bonnet.

The seconds dripped away. A pause which seemed para-doxically fast and endless.

Then it happened: fast and without warning. Boysie saw the taxi veer sideways on in front of them.

"Christ." The Jaguar driver high pitched. Something heavy came out of the darkness ahead and hit the windshield which frosted over as if sprayed with paint. The jolt as the driver hit the brakes.

Charles, in front, was very good. Calm, cool thinking. His hand punched forward breaking a hole in the frosted glass, battering out the fragments. There was a gun in his hand and he thrust it through the opening.

A metallic thump and a crunch. Charles screamed. You could hear the pain as he tried to pull his hand back into the car.

At the moment of the scream all the doors were wrenched open. Paul swivelled, gun up, but a strong black hand had his wrist, crushing like an iron shackle. The hand's twin wrapped around Paul's arm, above the elbow. Boysie heard the jolt of breath and the clatter as the gun fell into the road, just before Paul was dragged through the door. As he went there was a deep cracking noise from his shoulder.

Boysie looked back to where the driver had been. He was not there any more, and someone was releasing Charles' arm. As it came back through the windscreen, Boysie caught a glimpse of what appeared to be a mangled beetroot where the gunman's hand had been.

There were screams coming from the left outside and behind. Also to their right front. Snowflake Brightwater was hunched up in the embryo position, hands over her face.

Boysie looked beyond her through the door and saw a pair of immaculate striped trousers. The screaming stopped and Mister Colefax peered into the car. He was smiling.

"C-compliments o-of th-the B-board of T-t-trade," he said.

Boysie got out.

Charles lay unconscious on the pavement. He would not use his gun hand again for a long time.

Two large coloured gentlemen dragged the sagging Paul from behind the car and laid him out next to Charles. There was blood on his face and he would not use his arms and hands for at least a year.

Another brace of coloured gentlemen humped the driver from in front of the car and placed him alongside his companions. He was equally incapacitated.

Boysie heard Colefax say. "M-miss Bri-Bright-wa-water, co-could y-you g-get out of th-the c-car and g-go straight to the t-taxi."

Boysie, leaning over the Jaguar's bonnet, felt the great drops of sweat rise on his brow. Suddenly he could not breathe. He retched and parted with the bulk of his choc nut mousse, the delicious Plumrose chopped ham with pork and a fair proportion of Messrs Crosse and Blackwell's Pea Soup.

He gulped air, found his handkerchief and wiped his face. Colefax was standing beside him.

"Christ," said Boysie. "Sex, snobbery and sadism. You hit 'em hard."

"Th-they w-were g-g-going to-to k-k-k-kill y-you, m-m-man."

Boysie nodded. "How did you know?"

"W-we di-didn't. B-but y-you'll know w-w-we me-mean bus-s-s-iness. W-we ca-can pl-play ro-rough; and w-we're alw-ways n-near."

"Yes."

Colefax said he would have to stay and help clear up. One of the boys would run Snowflake and Boysie back.

"W-we're wa-watchin' y-y-you," said Colefax.

"I know."

They did not talk in the taxi. Boysie did not like what had happened. The world had erupted and for a while his nervous system had been expanded to maximum stretch. He was also aware of not being aware: he did not know the reason. That was a perpetual problem.

He managed a pirate airline company and the orders were given by Mostyn. While on company business he had met the sun goddess Miss Snowflake Brightwater. She had conned him. The cripple, Colefax, and the vocally unsuitable Frobisher, from the Ministry of Transport and Civil

Aviation and the Board of Trade, had pressured him into reporting on the dealings of his company. He did not know why. A brace of professional knock-off boys and their driver had come to execute himself and la Brightwater: he knew not why. Mister Colefax, from the Board of Trade, had come to their aid with a squad of extremely tough assistants. Why? Why? Double bloody why?

"Why?" he asked Snowflake Brightwater when they returned to the almost grotesque normality of her flat.

"I thought you could tell me. I knew Frobisher, Pester-licker and Colefax got mixed up in crazy situations. But all that bit was serious." It was the understatement of the night.

"I don't think they'll try again. Not after that. Will you be okay?"

"I'd rather you stayed until morning."

"I won't leave your side. After that, well, let's see what we can lay on." He crossed to the telephone and began to dial, hoping the number had not been changed.

It was a number in Harrow and Charlie Griffin answered almost at once.

"Mr Griffin?"

"I know that voice. Mr Oakes. How nice to hear from you again."

Charlie Griffin had acted for, and with, Boysie on many occasions, back in the old days. Griffin was a man who had stared death in the face from early in life and had come to terms with it. First as an undertaker; later as a perpetrator. But Boysie was not going to stop and think about that now. "You got any minders at hand?" he asked quickly.

"You in trouble again, Mr Oakes?"

"Minders, Charlie. Can do?"

"Cost you twenty-five a day and expenses. What do you want?"

Boysie gave him the address and a description of Snowflake Brightwater. He wanted the place watched back and front, nobody in or out except for himself and the lady. The lady was to be kept close when she went out. He also passed on the telephone numbers of the flat, his flat and the office.

"Shooters?" asked Griffin.

"With discretion. There's probably one okay-watch on both of us already. In spades I should think. They can be disregarded unless there's any funny business with the lady."

"Don't you worry your head about it, Mr Oakes, it's as good as done. I have access to only the best."

"I believe you."

"My minders are, if you like it, the Nureyevs of the profession."

"You're over-selling."

"Trade isn't what it was. I'm back in the old business if you're interested."

"What old business? Undertaking?"

"Not exactly. The bit that comes just before that."

"I'll bear it in mind. Call you in a couple of days."

"Any time."

"You know people, don't you?" Snowflake Brightwater said when he put down the telephone.

"Yes, I know people."

"I mean you know unpleasant people. People of violence."

"Like your mate Colefax, yes. I know him."

Snowflake Brightwater changed the subject. "It's going to be all right?"

"It's going to be sensational and we can sleep safely in our bed."

"And tomorrow?"

"Tomorrow is another year. Tomorrow is for decisions."

Much later, close to him and warm with afterglow she asked, "What do you really do?"

"I'm a jaded male model."

"Apart from that and satisfying available ladies like me."

"I help run this rotten stinking illegal airline. But not for long."

"I mean before that."

"Before that I was a salesman."

"Sell it to me anytime," she whispered, slipping away into dreams of great gentility far removed from the horrific realities.

Boysie could not sleep. His conscience held up his lids and the nervous trail, which had followed the events of the previous evening, flew through his consciousness like small evil demons.

By morning he had made up his mind for the hundred and thirty-first time. He could not prove Mostyn was actually responsible, but Mostyn was certainly the first cause of all that happened. Mostyn could go and fornicate among snakes. That was where he belonged. He, Brian Ian Boysie, Oakes would summon enough guts to tell Mostyn to do just that.

"Can I see you, Ada." He arrived briskly at the office.

Ada gave the other girls a knowing look and followed him into his private quarters. He turned and faced her, leaning against the desk.

"I want you to do a big favour for me."

"Anything: and I mean anything."

"That's good to know." He decided it sounded a shade self-satisfied. "Are Daddy and Mummy home?"

"No, actually they're in Spain." Puzzled.

"Good. What about your brother?"

"Toby's in Scotland."

"Great. Daddy's pistol range."

"Yes. Would you like to come and have another go? I mean by yourself, not with those two around." She jerked her head back towards the closed door.

"I'd love to do that, but not at the moment. Ada, the Diamondback revolver: the one I used when we came over. I want to borrow it, and some ammunition."

"What for?"

"Personal protection. I can't explain. It won't be used to break the law, I promise, and it'll be returned if Daddy or Toby show signs of coming home. I just need it for a while."

"All right. Nothing easier. When?"

"Now. I want you to go back and get it."

"Okay, but I'll expect payment. In kind."

Hell's teeth, not now, thought Boysie. The night had been exceptional and he was getting no younger. "It will be done," he said, nodding.

"Good." She leaned forward and kissed him, hard and

memorably sensuous on the mouth, her lips wide apart and tongue lashing around inside his stunned cheeks.

The kiss ended as abruptly as it started and, with a little wiggle, Ada walked to the door.

"Nice to know you're wanted," said Boysie.

"Keep you to it." She smiled.

It was comforting to have the Diamondback. Boysie carried it, loaded, safety catch on, in his hip pocket: not the best place for a small revolver, but without any kind of rig it was comfortable and handy.

The next three days passed uneventfully. The girls were all consistent in flashing their smiles, figures and thighs at Boysie, treating him as their lord and master, giving him the warm, glowing feeling of being fancied.

There were continual games. When Ada had to go out she always returned to a pile of frantic telephone messages from Steve McQueen. If Alma left the office she came back to cries of "Paul Newman called—FOUR TIMES." As for Aida, it seemed that Bill Cosby was always trying to get her when she was out. It was a fun office and on more than one occasion Boysie complained that the switchboard was liable to break down under the combined weight of calls from Steve McQueen, Paul Newman and Bill Cosby.

On the fourth morning, Mostyn came into the office, bright as a fox, garbed in russet worsted, a white shirt, brown silk scarf and a pair of brown brogues with strap and buckles. His links were tiny engraved silver reproductions of Scottish flintlock pistols, and he looked as though he had indulged in the full male grooming treatment.

"Well, well, Oakesie, that was an impressive performance. I have just been to the bank. Well done, lad, well done."

Boysie took a deep breath. "I want my bonus."

"You'll get your bonus." He smiled, sitting intimidatingly on the corner of the desk. "When's your Uncle Mostyn ever let you down?"

"You are not my uncle and I want my bonus now."

"What's this all about?" Mostyn's pleasant oil was cut

off at source. In its place was the brusque, tough man of extremes.

"I'll tell you what it's all about . . ." Boysie began.

"You gone chicken again?"

"You are a maggot, Mostyn." Enunciating like Steiger. "You do not give me pleasure."

"Take care, Oakes, or I'll have you, lad."

"You'll have nothing. I want my bonus. After that I quit, resign, turn in my bloody hand. I have had enough."

"Enough." It was a laugh.

"Yes, enough. Enough of you: you and your dirty, smelly, rotting, corpse-strewn, putrified ways."

"Facts, Oakes. What's been going on?"

"Going on? I don't mind making a public spectacle of myself by parading around Victoria Coach Station followed by a howling mob. I don't even mind humping other people's baggage. But when it comes to dark plots and threats and being almost murdered . . ."

"You exaggerate."

"Almost murdered: and the girl with me. I will not do it. For years you've had me on that bit of string. Offer Boysie money and he'll jump through any hoop. I've heard it, chum, and I've had it."

"Don't call me chum, Oakes. Sit down and listen because I have things to tell you that will turn your hair white."

Boysie sat. It was Pavlovian after years of service to Mostyn.

"You will stay," said Mostyn standing very near and almost speaking through his teeth. "You will stay for several reasons. First, you cannot be legally replaced with speed. Second, I have already entered into agreements with Excelsior to run at least two more trips. Third, you are getting bloody well paid and money's like a magnet to you, lad. Fourth, there are three young, pretty ladies out there just dying to drop their pants for you. You have that effect on some women, lord knows why but you do, and you love it. It is all milk and honey to you. You will stay because of these things."

Boysie slowly shook his head. "You can keep your money

and your willing available flesh. It doesn't matter any more."

"Wait." Mostyn held up a finger. "The two most important reasons. In running this caper you assist in screwing the government and that is something you won't resist."

"No dice."

"Lastly, Boysie, and most important of all: I thought you'd like to know about your father."

The unspoken; unthought. The small circle locked and kept at bay within. The hidden thing, hidden, for most of the time, even from himself.

"My father?"

There was the scent of salt spray and the wind dancing in across the Downs and the tall man with leathery skin.

"Your father, Oaksie."

"What do you know?"

Mostyn settled back on the desk. "All about him. I know what he did, where he went. I know who was responsible and I can lead you to that very man."

An irresistible bait. Feelings, emotions, welled up inside Boysie. He crushed them, holding on to the important ones, stifling sentiment and facing the hard realities.

7

Only Mostyn could have touched the old button, filled the mind with the thousand queries and wonderings.

Instinct urged Boysie to leap across the desk and grab his small slippery boss by the lapels. The nose to nose bit you saw on television melodramas; lifting the little man off his feet.

So you know huh?

Put me down.

Not until you tell me. Come on. Spill.

That was ludicrous. His mind opened up. Pictures of the village where he had waffled through a country childhood; and the tall man, gentle, quiet. Walks, friendship, then, out of the blue, nothing.

"You remember your father?" Mostyn was pushing it.

"Of course I remember." The tiny circle, closed by choice, now spinning wider. "But it's over thirty years." In a tiny rear mental partition, Boysie knew that the conjured picture was wrong. His father had been a short, rather thickset man who moved very quickly but did not smile all that often. Time warps. All childhood summers are recalled as sunlit and endless.

"You go on wondering, though, Boysie. For peace of mind the whole truth would help."

The dreams, about one every six months, and the unbidden memories, when the mind was at rest: suddenly the past reappearing.

"Thirty years is a long time."

"It's thirty-five if we're going to be accurate." Mostyn's voice grated like a rasp on metal.

"What's the difference?" In spite of the slight show of apathy, Boysie was hooked. He knew it. Worse, he was conscious that Mostyn knew. This was Mostyn's Sunday

Punch; the ace in the hole; the final thong, clamped around Boysie's heart, to be tugged bringing him to heel.

"How much *do* you know?" asked Mostyn.

There was a pause during which the telephone rang in the outer office. "Not much. He was a naval officer in the First World War and for a few years after. The sea was his passion, but I was brought up in the country, in the village."

"And he was there?"

"For most of the time. He was around. We were close. It was different though, he did not seem to do a job like other people; we weren't well off, but there was always enough; comfortable."

"The cottage."

"Yes, we lived in a cottage."

"He used to go away?"

The brown leather cases that seemed to fill that tiny room. His Ma upset. The tears in her big dark eyes and the old bone-shaker coming to take the man to the town and the railway station. Once Boysie begged to go with him. "Yes, he went away. It seemed for years, but he always came back."

"Didn't he ever tell you where he'd been?"

"No. Ma, my mother, said it was business and that we did not talk about business."

"Then he went away and didn't come back."

Boysie nodded. He felt nothing but the twinge of regret that he was sharing this with Mostyn. "Look, I don't want to talk about it. I was only a kid."

"What happened to Commander Oakes, RN (Retired)?" Mostyn smoothed the end of his nose with the middle finger of his right hand.

"It doesn't matter." Fighting away the desire to twist the key and have everything revealed.

"No?"

"Naturally one wonders."

"What happened, as you remember it?"

"He was away. It was summer. Two men came: in the afternoon. Ma was crying when they left. She called me in.

He had been in an accident, she said. The men had come to tell her."

"She ever tell you anything else?"

"At the beginning of the war she said that he'd been on important government business when he was killed."

"And you've treasured his memory." Mostyn made it sound like something you only did in secret.

Boysie nodded. "Of course. I was a kid. He was my Dad. A nice bloke."

"And you've wondered?"

"Of course. But I put it away. Stowed it. You can't go on being sentimental about someone you only remember as a child. Thirty years ago."

"Thirty-five. Nineteen-hundred and thirty-five. July. Commander Robert Oakes. Naval Intelligence, Boysie. That's what your old man was in. You followed in your father's footsteps. Only he wasn't a heavy. He did the sly, dark bits. Played the tourist in Europe. Took snaps. The only trouble was that his cover got severely blown in 1934. He should never have been sent out again. But his boss decided that he ought to have one more go. Churchill was yelling: telling the government that the Germans, now operating through Adolph Hitler Incorporated, were building an air armada. Your father's boss knew there was also a move to increase naval power. You with me, lad?"

Boysie, slumped in his chair, stared into space, locked into an afternoon yellow with corn and the green sensual sweep of the downlands. The two men were faceless. They had come late in the afternoon. He was home from school. Reading. A brown thick stiff-backed book with a picture on the front: horses and the clash of battle. *Sabre and Spurs* he thought it was called: about the Napoleonic wars. The car pulled up and his first reaction had been that it was Dad. But the men were short, in trilby hats.

When they left he heard one of them say something about his Ma being all right: a pension. Then came the nightmare and disbelief: the yellow day turned to shock and horror.

He looked up. "Yes, I'm with you."

"Under the Versailles Treaty, Germany was limited to

warships of ten thousand tons. But even in thirty-five they were planning the pocket battleships and Dönitz had his submarine force under way. Raeder had begun to work on Plan Z. Plan Z sounds just right for the thirties, eh lad?"

"Just right."

"Your father was good, Boysie. But he should never have been sent. They knew the risk. He left on July fifth. On July twenty-seventh they found him in a hotel room at Wilhelmshaven. His throat cut."

Boysie rose. "Mostyn, I really don't want to hear. I've got a picture of what he looked like to me. It doesn't mean anything any more." His voice belied the words.

"Killed by a system. The finger put on him by the one man who sent him out knowing it was odds on he would never come back. A stupid decision."

"So what am I supposed to do? Track him down and reap revenge like an avenging angel? You're sick, Mostyn."

Mostyn smiled. "My dear Oaksie. I only want to help."

"How do you know, anyway? How do you know about my father?"

"I've known for some time. I used to have access, you recall; access to libraries full of classified stuff. When it was a slow news day during the once and frozen Cold War I would browse. To be honest I came across his file quite by chance. After you joined us. It wouldn't have been of any interest to me otherwise. Now let's have the truth, Boysie. Wouldn't you like to come face to face with the man who sent your father on that mission?"

You live with something from childhood, keeping it under wraps, hiding it away, even from yourself: yet the questions were constant within the mind. How? Why? Where? What was he really like? What actually happened?

"Yes, I'd like to meet him," said Boysie. "It's not a question of revenge or anything like that."

Mostyn nodded. "It's the knowing, isn't it? I had an uncle disappeared in the thirties. No reason. No business worries. Nothing. There one day, gone the next. He was only an uncle, but I still wonder. So I know what it's like."

"No." Boysie rose. "No, Mostyn, you don't. You harboured the piece of knowledge. You found it and cherished it because one day you knew you might be able to hold it over my head. May your dreams decompose, because you've done it. Yes, I'd like to meet the man. I'd like to meet him because he could tell me what my old man was really like. I knew one side. He gave me immense pleasure. I would just like to talk to someone else who knew him."

"You shall, Boysie boy, you shall."

"When?"

"When we've completed this business."

"How many more trips?"

"Two. One on the fourteenth of next month. The fourteenth of May. The last on the tenth of June. If they are full, the Chief will have made a nice profit on his original investment. I will have done well, and you will have enough to set yourself up in some business."

"All right." Boysie sank back into his chair. He could not straighten his thoughts. "I'll tell you one thing, though," he said. "We're not having all that palaver at Victoria Coach Station again. I'm not going through that for an ornamental gold watch."

"I'll think about it," said Mostyn.

Colonel Peter Suffix took a pull on his cigarette, removed the holder from his teeth and regarded the dribble of smoke filtering from its mouthpiece.

"You say I can go on the fourteenth?"

"Yes. The fourteenth," replied his older companion raising a whisky glass and sipping. "Everything else will be delivered by the eleventh of June. Was the last consignment satisfactory?"

"I believe it's good. Tilitson and Knox report that training goes well. It should be a pushover."

"You really enjoy it, don't you?"

Suffix's weatherbeaten face cracked into a rare grin. "I wouldn't be in the trade if I didn't. Don't know any other way of life."

"What about morals?"

"Morals? Nothing to do with morals."

"I would have thought it had the hell of a bloody lot to do with morals. Thank you." The last to Suffix who had refilled the whisky glass. "I mean fighting other people's wars for them. The cause?"

"I'm not interested in the cause. I'm a professional soldier and when my own country gives me the old golden bowler then I'm for hire. Professionals are always for hire. Little dirty wars need big dirty people to fight them. To hell with the cause, if I didn't do it someone else would." He took another drag at his cigarette. "I've done a fair bit of it in my time. The last couple of decades have been good for mercenaries like me. Africa has bestowed riches on me."

"Ah well. I suppose it's all right. Wouldn't have been in my day. Loyalty, discipline, doin' what you were bloody told. Doin' your duty. King and country. Queen and country. Another spot of that Chivas Regal, if you don't mind."

After Mostyn left the office, Boysie telephoned Snowflake Brightwater and told her, cryptically, that he had a report to make. Would this evening be convenient?

"All my evenings are convenient for you. They are as small vacuums until you fill them."

"Everything okay?"

"Not a murmur."

"I'll call you this afternoon."

"I'd rather you called me darling."

Boysie busied himself with the affairs of Air Apparent: matters of great moment like getting the advertising copy ready for the small ads of the evening papers. At least it kept him from thinking, and the evening with Snowflake Brightwater would help.

The girls were in and out of his office all day and seemed to be vying for private moments with him. He was most conscious of Ada since the erotic kiss, and now Boysie wondered if they were playing some game. On one occasion Aida accidentally brushed his forearm with her breast as she passed and, whilst taking dictation, Alma had developed a tendency to sit in an attitude which exposed her all to

Boysie's gaze. It assisted in keeping his mind out of that emotionally sensitive area which Mostyn had revealed.

He let the girls go earlier than usual, remarking that tomorrow they would be selling tickets again, which always meant staying late.

The traffic was thick when Boysie got outside. He waited for a few moments in the hope of getting a cab to Eaton Place.

He was conscious of the Vauxhall pulling up, fast, but it was not until the rear door swung open, and the young man in the white Burberry leaped out and came towards him, that Boysie realised he was a target.

No time to take evasive action. The man from the car, big and extremely agile, loped up to him in a second. A hand clamping onto Boysie's right arm, at his tricep, just above the elbow.

"Come on, you're wanted." He was a man of around thirty and looked as though he meant business. For an instant, Boysie wondered if he should cause a scene—there were enough people about—but instinct rejected the thought. This one was playing cop.

There was no chance now, the man's hands were on Boysie's wrist and he was applying the Twist-Lock, Koga Method: nasty, painful and, what was worse, undetectable by the general public.

The Twist-Lock caused agony, particularly as the assailant was pushing Boysie's little finger hard across the other fingers, reducing strength and causing strain on the tendons.

"What the bloody hell's all this about?" Boysie exploded, but by that time he was in the back of the car and they were moving, snaking, threading and weaving through the traffic.

"Shut up and stay quiet," said the hefty man. His twin was on Boysie's other side and there was a similar specimen at the wheel. They could have been mistaken for cops. Or robbers.

Boysie's simple logic and experience told him they were up to no good. They had the sniff of Paul and Charles about them. The gut churn and desert at the back of the throat. His father ended up with a cut throat. With that

91

kind of luck running in the family he would probably finish with his head being blown off. The thought had a rough effect on Boysie's stomach. Then he felt the hard lump at his back. They had not even made an attempt to search him. The Diamondback was still there in his hip pocket.

He tried to concentrate on where they were taking him. It was a great pity, he thought, that Mr Colefax's gentlemen, or even Griffin's minders, were not keeping a leery eye on him as well as Snowflake Brightwater.

They were heading up the Tottenham Court Road by this time. A turn left, then one to the right. Another to the right. Boysie lost track.

Ten, fifteen minutes later, Boysie recognised the uncertain features of Finsbury Park. They pulled up before an unloved building. Across the street a pair of young dark men in 1950s Brando-type leather jackets did the Harpo Marx trick, holding up a Cypriot restaurant by leaning against it.

"Everybody out." He had the Twist-Lock on again.

"All right," yelled Boysie. "I'm not resisting. What the hell?"

The pressure was relaxed.

A narrow doorway. Steps, uncarpeted. They came to the first landing and, as they turned the stair, Boysie took action, wrenching free and leaping forward, his right hand moving faster than Lee Marvin in *The Man Who Shot Liberty Vallance*; faster than anyone; faster than Sammy Davis, even; the Diamondback came out as he swung round.

"Okay. Thread the fingers over the heads and quick."

The three paused for a moment and did as they were told.

"Higher," said Boysie, tipsy with power. They pushed upwards. It looked uncomfortable.

"Good. Now back up . . . er, down. Get down those stairs."

"What the devil's going on here?" slurred Frobisher from behind him. "Put that gun away."

Boysie lowered the gun. Looks of relief passed over the faces of the men on the stairs.

Frobisher was standing in a doorway. Behind him, in a shabby paper-strewn room, Pesterlicker rocked to and fro in his wheelchair.

8

"WHAT IN THE name of Satan's second cousin are you playing at?" Boysie leaned against the wall and let his wrath flow out diarrhetically. "You wave luscious lumps of lovely at me, then she spikes my drink. No sooner do I turn round than the both of us are heaved into a car and taken off for lead injections by a pair of killer maniacs. Then Mr Colefax and his singing swingers arrive and we get blood and guts all over the place; and to top it all you have me picked up by this bunch of oafish dolts. It's not good enough, Mr Frobisher, not good enough at all. You might have got people killed employing this type of person. I nearly shot one of them just to show it was for real. I could have filled them tight: tighter than an apple in a hog's mouth." It must have been the gun in his hand that inspired this last piece of old time Western talk.

"Come and have a cup of tea," mouthed Frobisher.

"Go down and wait in the car, boys." Pesterlicker's voice had not improved. "When you're involved in undercover work like ours you have to accept strange bedfellows, Mr Oakes."

"Strange bedfellows I don't mind. It's the feeble-minded, asinine, maundering attitude. You lot ask for bloody violence. If you wanted to see me why couldn't you send for me after some normal fashion?"

"It had to be quick," Pesterlicker grated.

Boysie went into the room and Frobisher closed the door behind them.

Boysie felt suddenly exhausted. The hand holding the Diamondback revolver shook and all the symptoms of post-terror took over: the stomach, pumping heart, constriction of the chest, sloppiness around the limb joints.

"You're playing at it," he said weakly. "Flaming amateurs playing cowboys and indians."

"You don't look too good." Frobisher was pouring out what appeared to be an impotent strain of China tea. "Milk and sugar?"

"Plenty of sugar." Boysie knew his *Pears Medical Dictionary*, having suffered the symptoms of most diseases in his time. He knew you had to have warm, very sweet drinks when in shock. Two abductions in a matter of days constituted shock.

"I'd better do the talking." Pesterlicker manoeuvred his wheelchair to a position near the desk.

The office was a shambles. Boysie could understand that. This lot obviously worked on a low budget, and if most of it went on strong arms such as those in the car below, or Colefax's impressive squad, there would not be much left over for the niceties of living.

Frobisher handed him the tea. It tasted like sweet warm water.

"We are concerned." Pesterlicker had very small eyes. Boysie had not noticed before.

"Concerned," repeated Pesterlicker.

"Good." Boysie slurped the tea. "About what?"

"About the situation with Miss Brightwater. You were to have paid her a visit tonight?"

"To make a report," Boysie got in quick.

"Mr Colefax's agents have pointed out that she is being watched from another source."

Boysie grinned. "Not to worry about that."

"This is most disturbing."

"No, it isn't. I fixed that one."

"You fixed it?"

"The minders. The other watch. They're there on my behalf."

"Are they now?" Pesterlicker sounded displeased. "On whose authority?"

Boysie's anger returned in a belch. "On my own bloody authority. That business the other night was bloody unnerving. Anyone can make a mistake, even Colefax's

94

commandos. I wanted a second string. Snowflake Brightwater's a nice kid."

"Do I smell orange blossom and rice?" From Frobisher.

"The pungent odour of romance." Pesterlicker was being really unpleasant.

"No. Just a good, healthy mutual attraction."

Pesterlicker raised a hand in peace. "Be mutually attracted by all means. But your watch will have to be called off. It confuses the issue."

"It confuses nothing."

"It confuses Mr Colefax."

"It's safer." Boysie knew the battle was lost.

Pesterlicker took the telephone from its rests and held it out towards Boysie.

"What's that for?"

"Call them off."

Boysie shook his head, he was not going to give away his contacts or sources in front of this garbage. "If you can assure me that she'll really be kept safe by Colefax then I'll call them off, but I'll do it in private."

"What other assurance do you need?" Pesterlicker spread his hands wide. "They saved both of you the other night. They're on the ball."

"Yes and we left them cleaning up the mess. There must have been a period when we were not being looked after. I filled that gap."

"You filled no gap. The Colefax System leaves no room for error. His methods of surveillance have been accepted as standard practice by government departments."

If you could not beat them, join them. "Okay," Boysie capitulated. "I'll call them off later."

Pesterlicker smiled. "You are not to go near Miss Brightwater tonight. In fact, if you try there may be trouble. There *will* be trouble until the other watch is removed."

Boysie looked passionately at his feet. His only hope for companionship and consolation that night had crumbled. Since Mostyn's bombshell, the big fear was the thought of being left alone to play only with memories. He nodded, eventually. There was no way round this one.

"What have you to tell us?" asked Pesterlicker.

Boysie told them of the two flights planned for the fourteenth of May and tenth of June.

Frobisher had a diary out and was making calculations with a pencil. They both looked worried.

"My gaffer says we're closing down after that."

They appeared to be even more unhappy. At last Pesterlicker spoke.

"From now on you must be very particular in your reports, Mr Oakes. For instance it will be essential for us to know exactly who is booking seats on these flights."

"Nothing easier." Boysie was cheered. It meant he would be able to take daily reports to Snowflake Brightwater. The girls always provided him with three copies of the booking list daily. Advantage to Boysie. "Anything else?" he queried.

"Lists of bookings and incidents out of the ordinary. The boys downstairs will take you home. In turn you will de-activate the watch on Miss Brightwater. We will inform her of tonight's change of plan." He sounded as though he had made up his mind, so Boysie did not try to argue.

Frobisher came down the stairs with him, giving instructions to the mob in the car. They seemed to understand Frobisher but remained just as silent to Boysie as they were during the drive down.

He made them drop him off in Kensington High Street. Bleakness descended as he walked into the Earl's Court Road. He decided that a bath, change of clothes, and a night around the town would be the answer.

The front door looked as shabby as the one which led to Frobisher's office. He went in, and up the stairs to the flat.

On his doorstep Aida sat, looking dejected.

"What are you doing here?" asked Boysie.

"Sitting on your doorstep looking dejected."

"I can see. Trouble?"

"Could be. What have you been doing?"

"Confidential business." He tried to make it sound sleazy.

"Oh her." Aida pouted.

"Come and tell me what's up." He unlocked the door, allowing her to precede him into the flat.

Once in, Boysie found himself reacting with his usual automatic mixture of gallantry and rakishness. But he was now conscious of it. He wondered whether this was a sign of the intrusion of age, or a conscience on behalf of Miss Snowflake Brightwater. She had become almost a way of life.

He helped Aida out of her coat. Underneath she still wore her crimson uniform tunic. The shape within had a stimulating effect. Conscience departed in a flurry of need.

Boysie sat her in the most comfortable chair and gave her the gin and tonic ("A nip of gin is all I take. Heavy on the tonic.") that she desired. Only when he was certain that all her immediate bodily comforts had been satisfied did he again ask what was wrong.

"It may be nothing, but I thought you should know . . ."

She really was a most attractive girl: the milk chocolate skin had a satiny texture while there was an edible quality about the small flared nose and good lips. A particular hunger swept over Boysie. He let his eyes drift down to the legs: pronounced calves, a long steady curve, proportioned thighs disappearing into her crimson skirt.

"Sorry," he said, "I didn't catch all that."

Aida told him that after everyone had gone that evening, she had returned to the office. A key left on her desk or something equally trifling.

"I got the key and I was just going to leave when I realised there was someone outside the door. Two men. East Africans I guess by the way they talked. One of them said, so this was the place it was all being run from. The other was all for using some kind of keys. Bones? Would that be it?"

"What did he say? Precisely?"

"As I recall it was, 'shall we use the bones?' The other one said to put the keys away."

"Yes." Boysie all knowledgeable. "Bones. Skeleton keys. Go on."

"They had a mite of an argument. The one guy wanting to come in, the other saying, no, all they had to do was identify the joint and make certain this Air Apparent Company was operating from there. They were only around for about five minutes. I waited for them to get clear before I left. I think I saw them when I got outside. There were two trying to get a cab. Man, they were big boys, but real big. All prettied up in light blue suits and rainbow ties."

Boysie nodded. They sounded like Mr Colefax's gentlemen. He made a mental note to report the incident. He could not do it tonight because of the restraint on visiting Snowflake Brightwater. He realised that he had not called off Griffin's muscle.

"You did the right thing coming straight here, Aida. Just give me a minute, I'd better make a call."

She smiled and settled back in the chair. With luck she was here for the duration.

Boysie went into the bedroom, picked up the extension and dialled Griffin.

"You can call off the minders, Mr Griffin. They've done an excellent job."

"You're sure, Mr Oakes? I mean it's no problem. If you want them a little longer you're very welcome."

"Enough is enough."

"If you say so, Mr Oakes." Griffin sounded sad. "Nothing else for me, I suppose?"

"Not at the moment." Then he remembered his father and the man Mostyn had promised him. There had been no thought of revenge at first, but a sudden puff of bitterness now filled him. "I might well have a hairy one for you before long. Around the middle of June."

"I'd be delighted, Mr Oakes. Delighted. Apart from the money it's nice to keep one's hand in, if you know what I mean."

"I know exactly what you mean."

Boysie went back into the living room where Aida was still snug, nursing her gin heavy on the tonic.

"Rewards." Boysie rubbed his hands together.

Aida raised her eyebrows. "For whom?"

"For you, Aida. You've shown great loyalty in coming here and waiting to tell me about what happened tonight. Rewards in food?"

"Food I could eat."

They ate Chinese in the High Street. Two number sixes, one number two, a double number twelve, a number fourteen and a number eleven.

It was very filling: especially the number twelve.

The conversation was scattered; Boysie asking Aida about home, and Aida telling him that home was really here, because her parents had come over when she was seven, so she thought of London as home.

They went on to talk about her painting but she swerved and brought the chat back to shop.

"You really going with that toffee-nosed piece you met at Gatwick, Mr B?"

The question was impertinent and surprising. Boysie looked at her, blank, flat-faced.

"Yes," he said, finally, choosing words with care. "Yes. Now and then. From time to time. Why?"

Aida smiled and dropped her eyes, the forefinger of her right hand drawing little ovals on the tablecloth. "Hadn't you noticed?" she muttered. "I got something going for you. In some circles they call it hot pants."

"Look, Aida, love. You're only a . . ."

"A young woman, yes."

As Snowflake Brightwater would have put it, Boysie was rent in twain. "I'm old enough to be your father. Anyway, I don't approve of affairs between the office staff."

"Who's talking about affairs? I don't want to go around with you. Anyhow, Mama would be furious. I just want to . . . Aw come on, Mr B, life's too short. Your place or mine?"

"Mine," said Boysie, feeling for his money to pay the bill. No fumbling.

"You've done it before, haven't you?" It was midnight and Aida lay criminally naked beside him.

"You're not exactly unpractised yourself." Boysie was sated. Batting it around with Miss Snowflake Brightwater was the greatest, but here was a special something to be remembered and savoured in old age.

"Getting late. Time I was home."

"You're not going out at this hour of the night?"

"It wouldn't be proper to spend the whole night here."
Aida was out of bed, and the sight of her unclothed stopped
Boysie's mouth. She took her time dressing, which was
another experience of visual delight.

"You want me to see you home?" He did not move from
under the covers.

She came and sat on the bed, beside him. "There's only
one thing I want from you, Mr B."

"Ah-ha." He leered.

"No." She put out a hand, to hold him off. "That's always
there when, and if, you need. I want you to take this." She
rooted in her handbag, bringing out a small card. It had
her name typed neatly in the top left hand corner. "I would
like you to write in the date and your signature, then keep
it safe and only produce it when I ask you to do so."

"Why?"

"There's no trick. I promise. You keep the card. Put it
in the bank if you wish."

Boysie was distinctly suspicious. However, he signed and
kissed her goodnight. Aida quietly left. She had produced
exquisite sensations for him and he felt much gratitude.

There was no sleep, however. With Aida gone, the
memories closed in and took over. Boysie shut his eyes and
immediately the picture returned. The slim man, laughing,
his face a tough sunburned colour.

At two o'clock, feeling ragged with new grief, Boysie got
out of bed, picked up his keys and went into the living room
where he took a strong belt of brandy. Between the kitchen
and bedroom doors was a high double-shuttered cupboard.
Selecting the key he opened the doors and stood back to
look at the clutter piled on the two shelves at the top of
the cupboard.

His larger belongings were stowed in the bottom section.
The battered multi-labelled tan Revelation that had
accompanied him on so many trips. A big green lightweight
suitcase that he knew was crammed with rubbish, the bits
and pieces collected during a roving life.

He removed the Revelation and the green case. Below
was a large polished mahogany box around two foot six

long, a foot wide, and eight inches deep. Boysie bent down and took hold of the pair of brass carrying handles attached to each side of the box.

Almost tenderly he carried it across the room to place it on the table. There was a large brass lock inlaid at the front, top centre. He looked down at his bunch of keys and again selected the correct one, inserting it in the lock and turning.

Slowly, Boysie opened the lid. The lid was a door into the long distant past. Even the wood and paint smell which rose from within evoked that other time and that other place.

Inside were three idential trays, well-fitting and stacked on top of each other, each tray about two inches deep. On top of each tray lay a carefully folded linen-backed paper. Boysie lifted the first tray out, took the paper and unfolded it.

Spread out it became a chart, roughly four feet by six, divided into squares, the land masses neatly painted in and marked: Belle Isle, The Cardinals, Quiberon.

Boysie looked at the tray: the immaculately carved model ships, each lying in its own pen. This was the chart and models, for the battle of Quiberon Bay, when Sir Edward Hawke chased the French, commanded by Admiral Conflans, under the great cliffs and among the rock-strewn seas of Quiberon in a heavy north-westerly gale.

Boysie took up one of the models, the *Royal George*, Hawke's flagship, from which he sent the signal *Form as you chase*. The detail remained superb and the paintwork looked almost new. Lieutenant Robert Oakes had spent hundreds of painstaking hours over these models. The ill-fated *Soleil Royal*, Conflans' ship which ran upon the Rouelle Shoal and was finally burned by the French; the seventy-four gun *Thésée*, hit by a squall with her lee ports open ready to fire. She filled with water and sank at once: only twenty-two survivors from a company of six hundred men including Conflans' best officer, Kersaint de Coetnempren. *Superbe*, into which Hawke's ship poured two salvos. She sank immediately. *Torbay*, *Dorsetshire*, *Resolution* and *Warspite*.

Boysie handled each model with care. It must have been three years since he had opened the box, for this was his only link with the dead man who had been his father. Even at this distance, the memory was incredibly sharp. The afternoons when the battle had been fought again and again, the man drawing a picture in words for the small boy: the gale creaming in the shrouds; the crash of gunfire rolling against the equal crash of waves; the strain-creak of the timbers.

The second tray was the Battle of the Nile: Nelson's *Vanguard*, Hood's *Zealous* and Foley's *Goliath*. *Conquérant* and *Spartiate*.

At the bottom of the box lay the most difficult of the battle games. Jutland, with its huge chart sweeping from the Skaggerrak to Scapa Flow, and the mass of ships, not so beautiful, yet sill created with delicate precision: *Iron Duke*, *Lion* (Beatty's flagship), the doomed *Invincible*, *Princess Royal*, *Queen Mary*, *Tiger; Lutzow, Derfflinger, Seydlitz, Moltke*.

Boysie stared at the chart. There was Jutland and Horn Reef, Heligoland and, he sucked in a strangled mouthful of air, *Wilhelmshaven*. He and his father had played many hours on this chart and with these ships; and on the chart was his father's final resting place.

He reached out and put his hand over the name gently patting the paper. So they cut your throat, Pop. They've tried to cut out my balls but I'll screw the bastards yet.

The same hell as before erupted in the office once the advertisement appeared in the evening papers. The telephones never stopped ringing, and the girls worked hard and happy. Aida, Boysie was pleased to note, seemed to treat him with a new respect, calling him 'sir' on every possible occasion.

"What gives with this 'sir' bit?" he asked her on the second morning.

"I have to show respect, don't I? After all I respect what you've got." She giggled.

Ada was pushing, constantly reminding him of his promise. In fact the whole business was becoming difficult. Each night he had to take a bookings list round to Snowflake Brightwater who, while adorable, was beginning to be a little demanding.

On the third day the name Peter Suffix appeared on the bookings list.

On the fourth, Boysie began to take the vitamin tablets recommended by his friendly chemist.

On the fifth, Mostyn showed up with the Chief in tow.

"Just thought I should take a look at the premises. Used to be a load of damn good, high class knocking shops in this area. Bloody fine people, the whores of Knightsbridge. But that must be before your time, eh young Oakes? All skinny-titted bits of bone with nothing to get hold of these days, like the three you've got out there." He indicated the outer office. "Wouldn't mind an hour or so with the fuzzy-wuzzy though, I must say."

Boysie winced and looked angry.

"If we have some whisky in perhaps the Admiral will . . . ?" Mostyn hurled a look at Boysie. The look was made up from a Sioux war arrow and a harpoon.

"No Chivas Regal, I'm afraid." Boysie smiled with vicious pleasure.

"Anything for me, my dear chap. Anything at all. Long as it's whisky. Become purely medicinal these days, you understand."

"I understand." Boysie uncorked the cheapest whisky they possessed.

With strained patience Mostyn and Boysie listened to the Chief's reminiscences: mostly of whisky and whores. It must have been fun at the time, but it was abominably boring to hear second-hand.

"Brain's gone rotten on him," commented Mostyn after they had poured the Chief into a taxi and waved him on his way. "Got another little job for you. Tell you in the office."

Once inside, Mostyn made himself comfortable in Boysie's chair behind the desk.

"It appears that it makes the charter people happier if one of our representatives toddles down to the airport and has a looksee round the aircraft from time to time," he said, like batter being poured onto a virgin's belly.

"Guess who's going to be the representative?" Boysie knew there were no prizes for that one.

"Well, what with you knowing all about aeroplanes and me having to trudge all the way off to black Africa." Mostyn's teeth were too clean to be true.

"Do I get special telephone numbers to call, and a small oblong of plastic ID?"

"All the fun of the fair." Mostyn tossed an ID card across the table: it simply showed that Brian Ian Oakes was the representative of Air Apparent Limited, and that he had authority to inspect aircraft chartered to Air Apparent by Excelsior Airlines. There were also permits to the apron and loading bays at Gatwick and Heathrow.

"I would imagine that the thirteenth would be as good a time as any. Evening before the flight's due out." Mostyn flashed an insincere smile on and off, quick as a blink. "Dull, ordinary sort of job, isn't it, old Boysie? Compared with the days when I used to send you out on more exciting tasks. You ever miss it?"

"You've never given me time to miss it. Do you ever listen to what I tell you? Since I've been a jolly rodgered pirate they've knocked the guts out of me."

"I trust it is the girls who are jolly rodgered," was all Mostyn replied.

That evening Boysie carried the news to Snowflake Brightwater.

"I can all but promise that the halt, the maim, and the aphonic will have much to say about your impending visit to the aerial gateways, my darling." Snowflake Brightwater leaned forward and kissed him tenderly on the chin. Boysie patted her knee, somewhat paternally as it had been a tiring day. First the Chief keeping an alcoholic eye on his investment; then Mostyn and his smarm; after which Ada had contrived to spend a lot of time in the office, during which she roused him fearfully.

"Our three bent and strange brothers," continued Snowflake Brightwater, "are most concerned about one name on your passenger list. A Mr Peter Suffix. They've been on to me about him all of a twitter."

"What do they want?" Boysie closed his eyes.

"A description. Better still, a photograph."

"No can do."

"Yes you can."

"How?"

"I will be around with my super sleuth miniature camera when you are seeing the voyagers off into the wide blue yonder."

He felt her hand on his knee. He kept his eyes closed and wished for sleep. Her hand rose and she began to tug gently at his zip.

"Boysie, darling, I am in need of attention. I require you to be lusty," said Miss Snowflake Brightwater.

Peter Suffix and his friend sat at a window table at Gennaros. Outside, the unpleasant Soho parade continued; the watcher, the watched, the young men in search of they knew not what, older shuffling men in raincoats that flapped around their legs; the garish near-beer spielers, the blue-pix pimps, and the gloves, dress, stockings, bra, G-string lay it all bare but do not touch, smoke-ridden clubs. The naked and the dead.

"I hope you're right," said Suffix digging his spoon into a large strawberry. He sliced it neatly in half, scooped up a little cream and sugar, then conveyed it to his mouth. "I sincerely hope so."

"I think there would have been trouble before this if Oakes and the Brightwater girl were engaged in a counter operation. It's purely an alliance for fornication. I've taken a lot of trouble on your behalf, Suffix. I stand to lose more than you. It was a foolish move to send your people in. Leave the security to me, dear boy. Had a lot to do with security and Intelligence in my time. Even had a file on you in front of me more'n once. So just concentrate on fighting the war you've fixed up for yourself."

Another strawberry found its way to Suffix's lips. "When it's over my name will be public. I just want it close and safe until then. Instinct still tells me I should have sent another lot in and got rid of them both."

"For heaven's sake, man. They are both being protected, but how can anybody know what it's all about? Eat your bloody strawberries and stop being so belligerent. Everybody's watching everybody else. But nobody has the truth."

"I have news." Snowflake Brightwater had taken to wearing a micro-kilt and no tights in the evenings. She maintained it was quicker. It was certainly more provocative. Boysie entered the flat, eyebrows raised to question her statement. "Have our loquacious trio decided to make a disc? Top of the Pops: *Pesterlicker and the Tongues of Fire.*" He followed her into the living room and took the large brandy she had ready for him.

"Sit down and a tale I shall unfold."

He sat.

Snowflake Brightwater sank to the floor in a delicate movement which ended in the lotus position. She looked up at Boysie and treated him to a smile which would have made the Invitation Waltz seem like the bum's rush. "We are to perform an assignment together."

"Who says?" A wary edge to Boysie's question.

"Mr Frobisher."

"Frobisher can go leap into the nearest sewer. I do what is asked of me and that's all."

"Oh, you don't have to do anything extra. You're going to Gatwick to inspect the aircraft on the thirteenth, aren't you?"

"Yes." Suspicious.

"So am I."

"Are you now? Frobisher say so?"

"Yes, my gentle sweeting."

"And did he provide documentation? You can't get in on mine."

"I have everything. Don't tell me you are blind to my allurements. They want me to go with you."

"What's the matter, don't they trust me? They think I'm going to climb aboard and soar off to pastures new before they get their pound of flesh?"

"Don't be so touchy. They simply feel that two heads are better than one."

"Not if they're on the same pair of shoulders."

Some time later Boysie asked her what she made of the whole situation.

"I don't know. Really I do not. I cannot make up my mind."

"You've worked for Frobisher, Pesterlicker and Colefax before, baby. Has there never been anything like this?"

"Not a thing. I have slaved in offices for them, checking on irregularities and the like. I've even been a decoy. I know they sometimes use unpleasant persons. But this one is strange."

"I can't figure it. You've never been involved in violence before? Like the other night?"

Her face changed colour, filtering to a dirty shade of parchment. "Don't remind me."

"You still scared?"

"Of course."

"With any luck it'll all be over next month."

"It's this month that concerns me. Your man . . . What's his name?"

"Mostyn."

"Mostyn tells you to go and look at the aircraft on the thirteenth. Frobisher says I have to hold your hand. It's almost as though Mostyn wants you to see something, and Frobisher needs me there as a witness. Perhaps they don't trust you, Boysie. You may be right."

"I shall be damned glad when the thirteenth is over and done with," mused Boysie.

9

Mostyn had made no new provision for picking up passengers. When Boysie broached the subject he merely gave an arch smile and said that they seemed to have managed well enough last time.

"But this is different. This time we've got to do it in daylight." The flight was scheduled out at noon on the fourteenth.

"Doesn't make it different, old lad. Calls for a little more ingenuity, that's all. Your problem. I'm sure you'll do wonders."

Boysie checked the booking lists and found that Suffix had elected to check in at Gatwick under his own steam.

"Your friend Frobisher'll have to fix that one," he told Snowflake Brightwater. "I've never put eyes on the man so I won't be able to finger him for you. Anyway I shall be fighting through the seething mob at Victoria Coach Station, won't I? If you want a snap of Suffix you'll have to make your own arrangements."

"Oh, what it must be to live such a purposeful and active life, Boysie, light of my heart. Running an airline must be so exacting."

"It's bloody hard graft."

Nevertheless, Boysie was enjoying himself for at least part of the time. When he thought of the stranglehold Frobisher and company held over him, his joy turned into a nagging worry; for he was only half certain that it was Mostyn they were after. It was very plain that if things came to a legal crunch it was B. Oakes who would have to carry the can. There was also Mostyn: he was to Boysie what the Black Death must have been to ordinary Joes during the Middle

Ages. Mostyn was the power behind Air Apparent. But what was Mostyn really at?

Yet, as far as the office was concerned, things swung. The aircraft was almost fully booked. Money rolled in: folding money, cheques and chink. The girls were happy. Tentative advances were made. Boysie held his ground.

Mostyn departed for Africa on the tenth and everyone sighed as though they had removed a pinching girdle. When Mostyn was in London you were never sure of his movements. He would not come near the office for days: then his descent upon it would be swift, soft-shoed and critical. If he paid a visit, routine went to pieces and they were all nervous for the rest of the day.

On the night of the eleventh, Boysie had a nightmare. When Boysie dreamed it was usually in technicolor. This one was technicolor, cinerama and stereo sound.

He walked along an endless beach, pebbles: the crunch of stones under his feet, a rhythm which got louder and louder until he was conscious of another person walking with him. He looked up. The man was with him but seemed a long way off. Tall, brown faced with a mess on his collar. Blood. Blood all round his collar. Crunch, crunch, crunch. Anxiety. Gunfire.

Ships off-shore. Sails bowing and flapping and the noise of gunfire. He was on the deck of some wooden fighting ship. Shot hitting the sails. The man with whom he had been walking lay on the deck. The deck unsteady under him. Shouting. Mostyn with a cutlass bearing down on him. Run. Running across the sea, only the sea was some kind of morass which dragged at his feet and Mostyn was behind. There were others coming from in front. A man in a wheelchair and others. Noise. He turned and a huge elephant rose from the sea, side on. It was draped in some red fringed cloth. Then the cloth rolled up. An horrific roar and the side of the elephant split open to form a massive, revolting pair of jaws. Sharp teeth. Red beyond. Red, red, red, red, dead, dead, dead, red, red, dead . . .

On the night of the thirteenth, Boysie picked up Snowflake

Brightwater at the Eaton Place flat just before nine.

Boysie had chosen his narrowest dark slacks and a dark green turtleneck to wear under a tight-fitting cord jacket. He did not want clothing flapping around. On his feet were canvas lace-up shoes with thick rubber soles. In the jacket pockets he carried a small torch, spare ammunition, a small leather case containing miniature screwdrivers, pliers and wire cutters. The Diamondback was snug in his hip pocket.

Activities in the past told him to be well prepared when Mostyn sent him on some casual expedition.

Snowflake Brightwater had also been sensible. A black pants suit and no dangling chains. The only bulges were natural.

Boysie had called Excelsior for a clearance during the afternoon. They drove out in Snowflake's Merc.

Activity at Gatwick was steady but not at crunch level. A tired, baggy-eyed young man in uniform and a cap, which said *Excelsior Airlines* across the front in gold, manned the Excelsior desk. Boysie flashed his ID and the young man yawned. "Yes. They said you'd probably look in. The aircraft's on the parkway, just off the apron, to the left of the terminal. She only got back from Cyprus this afternoon but I think they've finished cleaning and juicing her. Golf-Alfa, Echo, Bravo. She's open and the steps are down. You can't miss her."

He did not even ask to see Snowflake Brightwater's identification.

There was plenty of light from the arcs, on the apron and parkways; and it was chilly, a firm steady breeze blowing across the airfield. A British United BAC-111 was whining along the taxiway heading for the threshold, its engine noise carried to them on the wind, hitting their ears with a howl which made them cringe.

There were three big aircraft parked together. A VC-10, one of British United's fleet, and two 707s, one belonging to Air India, the second in the green, white and gold livery of Excelsior.

The steps were in place at the forward door. They walked round the aircraft once for the look of it in case anyone was bothering to watch. It seemed just like any other Boeing on the ground: cumbersome out of its element, impossible to believe that this long tube, with engine-weighted wings and a fin, had the ability to carry a couple of hundred people over thousands of miles, high above the weather.

On the starboard side the forward cargo door was open with a Ramp Veyor in position. An open gash, empty in the side of the aircraft. The elephant of his dream came bright and uncomfortable into Boysie's mind.

"What does that do?" asked Snowflake Brightwater indicating the Ramp Veyor.

"Saves airline companies employing a lot of guys to do the loading and unloading. You bring the baggage up in trucks. You have a couple of men loading the baggage onto the Ramp Veyor. When you set it going you get an endless belt . . ."

"There's an answer to that."

"An endless belt which carries the baggage up to the cargo hold where you have a couple of guys to off-load and stack it. Okay?"

She nodded. "Puts an end to all that humping."

It was an odd sensation to be alone in the aircraft. Normally you associate the cabins of stationary jet airliners with those moments of pre-takeoff stress: stuffed full of people, nippy hostesses being nimble with your hand baggage or telling you to sit down and fasten your seat belt: soothing piano and strings on tape to keep you cool.

They went up front, took a look on the boggling flight deck, peeped into the galley, crew rest area, forward loo, then walked up to the rear. Row upon row of empty seats. Tomorrow, Air Apparent's passengers would be filling the seats and the Boeing would be occupying air space to Africa. Dicing it to the dark continent, thought Boysie who did not like aeroplanes even when they were on the ground and unlikely to move anywhere.

They looked into the rear loo and walked forward again, the aisle floor rocking, minutely unstable, under them. Half way down Snowflake Brightwater bent to squint out of one side of the oval windows on the starboard side.

"Hey," she said quietly. "We've got company."

Boysie crouched behind her. From the window he could see a big red fuel bowser moving, almost cautiously, alongside the aircraft.

"Keep back and down," whispered Boysie, sliding into the outside seat and placing himself for a good view.

The bowser stopped and began to reverse. It was backing directly towards the Ramp Veyor.

"That man said it had been fuelled." Snowflake turned. "Sshsh, and keep well back."

The rear of the bowser was now almost over the Ramp Veyor. It stopped and four men jumped down from the cab, taking their time. Two of the men climbed up the Ramp Veyor into the cargo hold. The aircraft gave a tiny movement: a worried tremor. One of the remaining men was still standing by the cab looking around. Boysie lowered himself and stared out into the blackness which lay beyond the light illuminating the apron and parkway. Nobody in the terminal building would be able to see the bowser which was also shielded from the rest of the airfield by the Air India 707.

The man by the cab went round to the rear of the bowser and joined his partner who was fiddling with the stopcocks. They caught hold of one of the hand grips and pulled. Half of the rear swung away. The rear of the bowser was constructed so that it formed a pair of heavy double doors.

They could hear muffled conversation from below. Then the whine as one of them started up the Ramp Veyor. The two men on the ground climbed up and into the open hatch of the bowser. One of them now reappeared, jumping to the ground and assisting his mate with a long, coffin-like box. They unloaded the box from the bowser and placed it gently onto the Ramp Veyor where it was carried up out of sight inside the cargo hold.

The aircraft gave another gentle shudder as the pair of loaders in the cargo hold began to handle the box. By the time they had completed their job there was another box on its way up the Ramp Veyor.

The boxes were made of wood: stout, around five feet

long. Medium sized coffins with rough rope carrying handles at each end. Boysie had only seen boxes like that used for one purpose: packaging rifles and similar weapons.

The team worked for around three-quarters of an hour, loading some forty boxes, followed by a number of smaller, more square boxes.

Finally the whine of the Ramp Veyor stopped. The pair came out from the cargo hold and began to uncouple the Ramp Veyor. From the noises Boysie guessed they were closing the cargo hold door. The other men had shut the doors at the back of the bowser and one of them disappeared out of sight under the aircraft.

Boysie heard the footfalls on the gangway steps.

"Quickly, and as quietly as you can. The rear loo," he whispered.

Snowflake followed him up the aisle and by the time the loader arrived on board, they were jammed tight together in the narrow rear lavatory, the door partially open.

The intruder walked the length of the aircraft and came to a halt outside the lavatory door. They could hear his breathing, and Boysie was conscious that he was holding his own breath, Diamondback out and ready in his right hand. Snowflake Brightwater's face betrayed terror. Boysie's little finger to his lips.

The man stood still for around half a minute, then began to walk back to the front of the aircraft. They heard him go right forward onto the flight deck before leaving the way he had come.

They waited for a couple of minutes before coming out of the lavatory. A quick glance from the starboard windows showed that the bowser had gone.

You take no chances in a situation like this. It was conceivable that one of the men was still there, on the ground below.

Boysie motioned Snowflake to stay where she was. Still clutching the Diamondback, safety catch off, he walked quietly to the front of the aircraft and stood in the doorway for a moment before descending. There did not seem to be anybody near the aircraft. Boysie circled the machine. The cargo door was closed and the Ramp Veyor stood a little away from the aircraft. Everything else was normal.

Boysie was red with anger. It was as though the whole of his mind and brain was suffused with a violent crimson fury. Snowflake Brightwater drove; and they had hardly exchanged a word since getting into the car.

Mostyn was all Boysie could think of in the centre of the crimson whirlwind: hurricane red with Mostyn as the eye. There was no doubt in Boysie's mind or heart. Mostyn's game was illegal arms dealing and Air Apparent simply operated as a means of moving weapons out of the country. If something went wrong, Boysie Oakes, king of the airline pirates, would face not only the civil actions rising from the intricate running of Air Apparent, but also the criminal charges of smuggling illegal arms.

The fire within cooled to ice as he thought about the complexity of the operation. The weapons and ammunition had to be brought to some central point; they had to be loaded into the bowser; the bowser had to get to the aircraft. There would be bribes and fiddles. At any point in the chain a link could break, and who would be the one to be dropped straight into the fertiliser? Joseph Mugging Oakes, and on that day he would not be wearing his brown suit.

"Did those boxes contain what I think?" asked Snowflake Brightwater.

"It depends what you think they contained."

"Automatic rifles, machine guns, sub-machine guns, pistols, revolvers, grenades and the wherewithal to use such things."

"Yes." Curtly.

"And we report this to our superiors?"

"You report it to Frobisher. You also say to him that I want out now, this minute. Sooner. I don't want to take the responsibility."

"He won't like that."

"I don't suppose he will, but I am taking an independent action, and I do not wish to be associated with Air Apparent any longer. Finished, paid off, closed. I wish my quietus to make with Air bloody Apparent. Pig Dung."

"What?"

"A vulgarism used in my youth instead of the expletive shit."

"Oh I see."

Snowflake Brightwater dropped Boysie at his flat. She said that she was anxious to get on and make the report as quickly as possible.

Inside, he emptied his pockets and stared at the assorted objects. All my danger man gear, he thought. Aloud he muttered. "Dad, old Dad, what would you have done?"

Danger man, Christ I was scared when that geezer came on board.

He dialled Griffin's number.

"You busy?" he asked curtly when Griffin came on the line.

"Trade's terrible, Mr Oakes. Must be the credit squeeze still biting."

"I might have some work for you."

"I'm sure we'll give you every satisfaction." Griffin brightened.

"You'll be dead satisfactory." He gave Griffin his new address. "Six tomorrow evening?"

"Well, now, Mr Oakes, I don't usually like meeting people in a confined space."

"Come off it, Charlie. After all we've been through together."

"Very well. Six o'clock tomorrow."

An hour later Boysie was in bed with one of Frederick H. Christian's *Sudden* books and friend Sudden was sure getting stuck in: he had hornswoggled that pesky dude mine owner and shot up a couple of outlaws who were planning to rob the stage. Now Sudden dealt a bit of rough justice to those no good brothers who were out after getting their hands on the clean-limbed, hard-working rancher's land. Boysie liked Westerns. He could get involved without getting hurt.

The telephone bleated.

"Yip?"

"Boysie darling."

"Snowflake angel."

"You sound in a better humour than when I left you."

"Yes, well I'm working on it."

"You were most grouchy and there I was all frightened. It's no fun to be locked in an aeroplane loo with some maniac wandering around."

"I know. I was there."

"My hero. I have messages for you."

"From the Trinity?"

"All three. Very heavy messages, Boysie. You are to do nothing of your own accord. They say that would be fatal. Mr Pesterlicker stressed the word *fatal*."

"You still there, my sweet?" asked Snowflake Brightwater.

"Palpitating," replied Boysie truthfully.

"They also said I was to tell you not to worry. You are to do anything your man tells you without question, and you must show him no animosity. You will carry no blame."

"It's all very well them saying that."

"You can see them and get their confirmation in person if you wish."

"I do not wish."

"I do wish I was with you."

"Yes," Boysie reflected.

"What are you doing?"

"I told you. Palpitating."

"Yes, but where?"

"In bed."

"Oh, my. Palpitating in bed. Do you think we might palpitate in bed in the very near future?"

"I'm certain of it," grinned Boysie.

The farce at Victoria Coach Station was as bad as before. Worse if anything, for they got entangled with a girls' school on a day trip, shepherded by penguin nuns with no sense of direction.

A bald-headed man, aching to be on his way to Africa, found himself back in the Lower Fifth, while two maiden ladies, travelling to meet their long lost brother in Johannesburg, were almost swept into eternal virginity within the Order of Saint Martha Without Broom.

Boysie caught sight of Snowflake Brightwater at Gatwick, but they had agreed not to have any contact. She appeared to be lurking with considerable effect.

The red anger returned as Boysie watched the 707 rise gracefully into its native air leaving thin dark trails behind. He thought of what he knew was on board: the fact that he was carrying a weapon for his personal protection did not seem to make any difference. The stuff on that aircraft was for disruption, revolt, violence, rebellion. That was the only reason you smuggled arms and weapons. Weapons spoke a special language. Universal. The language of death and disease and famine.

He thought of Mostyn and how he hated the strumming evil that throbbed in the man. Mostyn and his superior manner intimidated people. Now he was adding to his gallery of nastiness, for the weapons would intimidate far better than Mostyn and his slippery ways.

He thought of Pesterlicker and Colefax and wondered what they were really about. He also wondered, for the umpteenth time, if he could trust them.

He thought about his father, and Boysie's determination became stronger.

He thought about Snowflake Brightwater and just wondered.

He thought about Charlie Griffin and recalled that he had a meeting with him that evening.

Charles Griffin was a nondescript man: thin faced, wearing glasses. To the outside world he looked faded. You would not have taken a second look at him. This was an asset to Griffin. He knew it and liked to keep it that way.

He rang Boysie's bell precisely on the dot of six.

"Dead on time." Boysie opened the door.

"We all will be, Mr Oakes. That is for certain. When our time comes it will be accurate. Trust in it."

"I do, I do. Have a drink?" He ushered Griffin inside and took the light raincoat.

Griffin stared about him rubbing his hands. "I don't mind if I do, Mr Oakes. Don't mind if I do at all. A spot of rum if you happen . . ."

"Yes I have rum. Good black rum from the Caribbean."

"Nelson's blood." Griffin smiled benignly. "Always partial to a spot of rum. When I was in the undertaking trade we always had it during the winter: after the interment of course. Never drank before. Always best to be steady, grave and sober, though I did hear of one time when a parson turned up well seasoned for an interment. Fell into the grave and climbed out making blasphemous comments about the doctrine of the Resurrection. Not good. Nice little drum you got here."

"Not as good as some we've known, Mr Griffin. Cheers."

They saluted each other with alcohol, and Boysie offered Griffin a chair. When Griffin was settled, Boysie took the chair opposite.

They smiled at each other.

"Come on now, Mr Oakes, we've known each other a long time. What's on your mind? Or should I say who's on your mind? If you'll excuse my little joke."

"Know anything about illegal arms dealing?"

The smile dropped from Griffin's face. "Now Mr Oakes, have a care. That's not a nice business."

"I know. But I'm still asking, because you know a lot of people."

"I know it goes on. I know how some of it is done. But I know nothing if you follow me. I regard arms smuggling in much the same way as I regard the White Slave Trade."

"But there isn't a White Slave Trade any more. Or a black one come to that."

"You would be surprised." Griffin laid a bony finger alongside his nose.

"You're against it anyway?" One had to be precise with Griffin—it was all part of the business.

"Absolutely."

"Then you'd not be adverse to taking on a small contract to deal with someone who's been at it?"

"Delighted. Just supply me with the details."

"Mostyn," said Boysie with venom.

Griffin's jaw dropped in a spectacular manner. "Never."

"Mostyn," repeated Boysie.

"Now look here, Mr Oakes, you know my rules. We've both worked for Mr Mostyn in the past. Been colleagues. I never terminate former colleagues, you know that."

"I know, but I wondered in this case . . . ?"

Griffin wrapped himself in thought. "The evidence would have to be pretty conclusive."

"I'll provide the evidence."

"Once I have considered the evidence then I will give it my attention."

"That's all I need to know, Mr Griffin. There will be another as well."

"Two?" Griffin raised his eyebrows. "Who's the second?"

"I don't know."

"Ah. It's always better to know."

"I get that information from Mostyn so I can't let you do Mostyn until I know."

"A very complicated situation, Mr Oakes, but I'll do my best to oblige."

Griffin left around seven o'clock. Griffin never overstayed his welcome.

Snowflake Brightwater telephoned at seven thirty. "Have you time for a quiet and private tête à tête?" she asked.

"I was just thinking the same thing," said Boysie who had shaved with care and anointed his jowls with the pungent spices of *Aramis*.

"I wish to talk business, but that will not take too long," purred Snowflake Brightwater. "As they say, all work and all that."

When he arrived at the flat she was wearing the long white gown made up of many layers of diaphanous material: the gown with which she had covered her body on the night of Boysie, the brandy and the Micky Finn.

"You looked lovely at the airport."

"I thought you hadn't noticed. You looked nice as well. I love your flat cap. Most official and avant-garde."

"I shall wear it at fancy dress parties when I go as a British Rail avant guard. Now what's the business?"

"I took some very pretty pictures." Snowflake crossed the room and returned with a photograph and a book. "The tricky trio are in possession of most of the prints, but I kept one specially for us. This," she held out a colour print, "is Peter Suffix: the person Frobisher and his friends are so agitated about."

Boysie took the photograph. The man was leaning forward over a check-in desk and Snowflake had got him from head to waist, full face. He looked tall, the face bronzed and he was wearing a denim battledress jacket with a coloured scarf in the neck. A silver medallion hung from a thin chain around the neck.

Boysie scowled. The features were familiar.

"Suffix," repeated Snowflake Brightwater. "You recall him now?"

"I know the face and the name but I can't . . ."

"He got a lot of publicity in the sixties. Much mud-throwing. He even wrote a book." She held up the copy in her hand: *The Mercenaries of Europe* by Colonel Peter Suffix.

"Of course. I saw him on television once. We had a file on him in the old department. Christ, he was once a possible target." He clamped his mouth shut. "I never said that. I just contravened the Official Secrets Act."

Snowflake Brightwater snapped a smile on and off: quick as a kingfisher in August. She tapped the dust jacket of *The Mercenaries of Europe*. The jacket design consisted of dark black and red swirls, clouds: a fire in the wake of bombs. In the centre was a black drawing, a cobra with its head raised spitting fire. She tapped the cobra. "That's Suffix's personal device. Men serving under him wear it as a flash on their sleeves. If you look at that photograph through a magnifying glass you'll see he's got it on the locket round his neck."

Boysie nodded. He had his eyes closed trying to remember all he knew about Suffix. "You've obviously been checking up on him. Tell me when I go wrong. Colonel Peter Suffix. Professional soldier. Regular Army. Served with Parachute

Regiment. Axed in the late fifties and given the golden bowler. Kicked up a big stink in the press and offered his services to the highest bidder. Served as a mercenary in almost every major conflagration since then. And quite a lot of minor ones. Revolts. Specialist in assisting military coups. Responsible for some hideous carnage in the Congo. Some Tory MP once called him, 'Undoubtedly a gallant gentleman, but unfortunately a very dangerous one.' Anything else?"

"Yes. Rumoured to have most recently fought for Ojukwu in Nigeria."

"And our flight is running into Angola. Mostyn and Suffix. It makes sense. Mostyn would sell his soul and not give a hang who got hurt. Weapons shipped out illegally for some kind of African stir up with Suffix in the lead. Mostyn gets the loot. The bastard. The four-letter effing, rotten . . ."

Boysie saw the teletype message the moment he entered his office the following morning. It sat square in the middle of his desk. The nasty nip in the guts came and went unheeded. He covered the distance between door and desk in three strides.

When he finished reading the message, Boysie shouted for Aida. He called four times: loudly, the name almost strangled at the back of his throat.

The teletype message read:

CHARTER FLIGHT E THREE-THREE-EIGHT GATWICK–LUANDA MADE EMERGENCY LANDING AT OTUKA THIS AM STOP FUEL SHORTAGE STOP DELAYED TWO HOURS SO RUNNING TWO HOURS BEHIND SCHEDULE STOP PASSENGER PETER SUFFIX DISEMBARKED LEAVING AIRCRAFT AT OTUKA STOP.

10

ETSZIKA COVERS AN area of approximately two thousand five hundred square miles. Its seaboard stretches for fifty or so miles along the western coast of Africa. This small tract of land has the Republic of Gabon as its northern neighbour and the Republic of the Congo (Brazzaville) to the south. The border between these two countries dissects Etszika's frontier in the east.

Etszika was a small British colony, alone midst the French territories of Gabon and the Congo (once part of French Equatorial Africa), until it was granted independence in 1959. It then became the Republic of Etszika.

The people of Etszika are derived from two tribes, the Etsziki and Bowoni, and the country's economy depends largely upon timber and agriculture, though in recent years the Etszikans have looked more and more towards light industry.

Etszika boasts four small, modern cities; its capital, Otuka, being the largest, is situated on the coast.

Etszika has a president who is elected for a term of seven years. The National Assembly, a one-house legislature, has thirty members.

There is an existing defence and aid treaty with Great Britain. The people are of a friendly and happy disposition and . . .

Boysie stopped reading and flung the encyclopaedia onto the desk. "Aida, I don't want to know about Etszika's people being happy and of a friendly disposition. I want to know about its president and the political brains around him. I want to know of plots and intrigues and all the little disturbances. The inner scene. Dig?"

"They've got an office in London. Shall I give them a call?" Aida tried to be helpful.

"No, for God's sake don't do it with officials. Stealth.

Now think, do you know any Etszikans, or whatever they call themselves, in London?"

"Nope."

"Well, go and think. Do your best."

Snowflake Brightwater called an hour later.

"Your presence is required."

"For what?"

"They wish to talk with you."

"I can't just up and leave my desk and come running when they see fit to call. I've got a job to do, honey. Where?"

"Here. My place."

"When?" With the weary tone.

"Now. As quickly as you can."

"What do they want?"

"I think it's to underline their last instructions," she whispered. "They don't want you to blow anything before they are ready."

"I'll be there."

Boysie took a truculent attitude with Frobisher, Pesterlicker and Colefax.

"I hope this isn't a wild goose chase. I really must point out that I've got an office to run."

"We send men for you and that's not right . . ." began Frobisher.

"You must realise that you are, to some extent, in our employ, Mr Oakes." Pesterlicker was speed testing his wheelchair in circles round Snowflake's living room. "You did not like the way we called you last time. Now we have shown tact, respect, gentleness even. We wish to see you. We have called you to this lovely lady's beautiful apartment. What more can we do?"

"Y-y-yes, M-man, y-you're ge-getting t-too up-up-up-up . . ."

"Tight?" rasped Boysie.

"T-tight." Colefax nodded.

"Well, it isn't easy. I don't like this business at all."

"Do any of us?" Pesterlicker screamed to a halt in front of Boysie, making him flinch. "You *are* getting uptight and

123

it *is* obvious. You are concerned about being involved in shipments of illegal arms. You are nervous about Colonel Suffix. You are worried about the involvement of your own employer: the man Mostyn."

"Stuff Mostyn."

"That is exactly what you must not do. That is why we've sent for you. When Mostyn returns you will behave towards him as you would to your closest friend. You will do nothing that might alarm or alert him. Have trust and faith."

"Me," said Boysie, his mouth wide. "Me, be nice to Mostyn? He'll smell a rat."

"We simply want you to behave normally. Can we have your promise on that?"

Boysie groaned. Promises, promises. He had to promise Mostyn that he would continue to operate Air Apparent. Mostyn in turn promised Boysie's father's ex-boss on a plate. Now, more promises.

Boysie raised his fingers in the old Wolf Cubs salute. "I promise that at all times I will do my duty." It may not have been quite right but it was what came back into his memory.

Aida followed him into his office when he returned.

"Got it," she said with triumph.

"Got what?" Everything was crowding in and Boysie had temporarily forgotten about Etszika.

"Mama knows someone in the Etszikan Embassy. I got to talk to him. Said I was doing a paper of West African politics."

"And?"

"They are worried about the president. President Anthony. Apparently he's a good old man brought up in the ways of Western democracy."

"No wonder they're worried."

"Listen. He was re-elected for his second term of office in 1966. But, like everywhere else, there is change and protest. There are those who think he's too weak."

"Members of the National Assembly?"

"Yes, some there, but especially people in the army. There is a small army: around nine hundred men. One of President Anthony's most outspoken critics is General Bushway, Commander of the army. In the London Embassy, they fear that he may attempt a military coup. But some say the army is divided, that Bushway would need much help from outside."

Boysie nodded. It made sense. However, it was really none of his business. Frobisher and company had already warned him off. He thought about the next flight, due out on June tenth. Would that be heavy with arms and ammunition as well? Who would be on board? Ordinary passengers bound for Luanda and from thence to Johannesburg? Or men like Colonel Suffix? Men with military ability selling themselves? There was a ready market for those who could shoot straight and had good stomachs. Christ, thought Boysie, we're back to where I started. Mostyn's always been in the hire and fire service for liquidators. He's simply doing it on a larger scale now.

The camp was some twenty miles from the airport at Otuka: away from any main road, deep in the forest.

The two black officers who had met Suffix at the airport went with him to the camp: one sitting in front with the driver, the other in the back with Suffix.

Suffix was pleased to note that the man in the back had a Colt .45 automatic on the seat between them. Suffix was unarmed.

You could only reach the camp by travelling along the narrow, hard, rutted track which wound and dipped through the forest. It was only just wide enough to take the car.

In the forest they were stopped three times. The men seemed to rise from the road in front without warning. Suffix used his eyes well. He could feel the weapons on him from the trees. But he could not see them. That was good. The task force was being trained well.

When they reached the camp Lieutenants Tilitson and Knox were there to meet him. They took him to his quarters:

a small hut with a veranda. There were two rooms: one for sleeping, the other for day use. Facilities for washing were outside. He would share the field latrine with the other officers.

As soon as he settled in, Suffix unpacked his gear. Tilitson had brought over his webbing belt and holster, the service .38 which he preferred to the Colt .45, and his olive green beret. On the side of the beret was the silver embroidered cobra spitting fire. In this part of the world Suffix was often known as The Cobra.

The General arrived late in the afternoon.

"Peter, my old friend, it is good to see you. Now I feel safe." He was a massive man. Thirty-seven or thirty-eight years old; at least six feet tall with great bull shoulders and a fine expressive head.

"It is good to see you, sir. We have much planning. Much talking to do."

"Indeed. Things are not good. I am watched in the city. The officers loyal to the President are forming a tighter circle than I had thought. However, they think they are safe. There's bound to be some complacency, and complacency is to our advantage."

"Well, sir, we cannot act until after the eleventh when the rest of the equipment arrives."

The General made an impatient sound. "That is what worries me. I don't really like holding it that long. Still, the night of the eleventh would be ideal. There is to be a party at the President's residence. They will all be there. It would be easy."

Suffix clicked his teeth. "Then we'll have to adapt, won't we, sir."

"What the devil gives with the Otuka bit? That really bugs me. It's happened twice." Boysie had managed to control himself during the hour that Mostyn had spent in the office.

Mostyn's return was, as usual, silent, creepy, unheralded.

Now Boysie felt he must at least face his employer with one question.

"Oaksie. Don't get so upset." Soothing. "What do you mean, the Otuka bit?"

"It happened on the first charter. It happened again last week. The aircraft made an emergency landing at Otuka. Why?"

Mostyn's smile was really a sneer. "Because that's the way we planned it, lad."

"Then why plan it that way?"

"Try flying a 707 all the way without making a juicing stop. Look at the map, lad. You can't get there in one hop. We do not want to draw attention to the trip, nor do we wish to invite trouble. Excelsior had a tacit agreement with Etszika: facilities for juicing at Otuka. The emergency landing signal's simply for the look of the thing. Don't you listen to anything they tell you at Excelsior?"

Boysie kept back his rage and held his tongue.

"Anyway," continued Mostyn, "there's a lot to do. We've got under three weeks to June tenth and I want a fully-booked aircraft. Once that's over we can all breathe out and pass on the germs. I've brought the tickets down for you. Now get selling."

It was becoming routine: a regular, normal operation. This time it seemed more enjoyable than ever to Boysie because he knew it was simply a matter of days. Either the flight would go as planned and they would catch up with Mostyn later, or, somehow, Frobisher and the others would move to stop things before the flight left. He began to acquire a sense of the fact that it was out of his hands. He even gave up thinking about the decision he would have to make: whether to use Griffin.

The only regret was having to tell the girls of Air Apparent's demise. He put the moment off daily, telling himself that it would be easier tomorrow. It never was.

The weather was good. Snowflake Brightwater remained perfect. Frobisher, Pesterlicker and Colefax kept their distance and Mostyn did not often show up at the office. Boysie even started to feel secure. Until the sixth of June.

It was Saturday and the office was closed. Boysie slept late and was not even dressed when the bell rang.

Mostyn stood in the doorway, his face like thunder.

"It's my day off," said Boysie in his I-brook-no-arguments voice.

"My heart bleeds." Mostyn advanced, closing the door behind him. "We have a problem."

"You have a problem."

"Excelsior's let us down."

"So we cancel the trip."

"They haven't let us down that badly, but enough to get me out of bed and put me in a menacing mood, Oakes. Excelsior can provide the flight crew and also an aircraft on the tenth. They cannot provide a cabin crew."

"Your problem . . ." Boysie started. Then he stopped abruptly. He recognised the look in Mostyn's eyes and the news slowly hit his brain, was unscrambled by the computers, and translated into answers. "Oh no. That's not part of the deal. I don't do that for anybody."

"I have solved the problem." Mostyn pushed close to Boysie. "And it's got to stay solved because I'm off to Africa tonight. I have told Excelsior that we will provide our own cabin crew. One steward and three hostesses. You get to tell the hostesses."

Boysie closed his eyes. In the foreground of his mind there was an elephant with its side splitting open into a gaping wounded mouth. Great teeth. White. Red. Blood red. The roar.

"That's right. You can see plainly on this map. The president's residence takes up one side of the Square of Independence, which lies directly behind the Square of the Assembly. In the Square of the Assembly we have the House of Assembly and the Government Administration Building."

The General spoke quietly. It was their third meeting, sitting in Suffix's day room. An armed guard was with them, and two soldiers were posted in front of and behind Suffix's quarters.

"I thought from the start that the layout was favourable." Suffix looked down at the large scale plan of Otuka spread before them. Some areas—the government buildings, main post office, radio and television stations, the airport—were ringed heavily in red pencil. Suffix's eyes were centred on the area just indicated by General Bushway. Carefully he began to make more pencil marks, sealing off the three road entrances to the Square of Independence and the Square of the Assembly. "I want to get the army situation quite clear in my mind. You have isolated the regiment which is loyal to yourself?"

"The one that will obey my orders, yes."

"And the remaining two regiments will be out of the capital?"

"Tomorrow they leave for exercises in the north. Forty miles away."

"How quickly can they get back into the city?"

"In theory, within two hours. The roads are good. In practice, a good deal longer. The transport officers of both units are loyal to me. I also have several loyal officers and technical men."

"So we can be certain of a delay of up to . . . eight hours?"

"Six."

Suffix nodded. "It should be enough. Now security. What is the situation there?"

"The police force will obey the military. There is no doubt about that; and it will be my military in the first instance. I have also completely infiltrated the NSA, National Security Agency. There are only thirty of them. Eighteen are mine."

"Any trouble and the other twelve . . . ?"

"Quite." The General spread out his fingers. "Any trouble and they will be killed." A statement.

Suffix was pleased. In matters such as this there was no room for hesitation or squeamishness. Suffix knew why he had been hired. The General was a military officer in rank only. The man was an idealist; a politician not a soldier. Suffix would be the one in charge of the army that finally emerged. He would also be the one who had to make the military decisions on the ground.

"What other security aspects are there?"

The General leaned back in his chair. "Your own country. They are anxious that Anthony remains in power. From the activity you have experienced in London you know that they are alert. They have people in the country . . ."

"I don't think that lot'll want to shoot it out."

"No. But the Government Security Corps will."

"Uh-hu. And they are?"

"Virtually the president's personal plainclothed body-guard. There are twenty of them. Their office is in the Government Administration Building and, I should imagine, they will have between seven and ten men on duty at the residence during the reception."

"Any chance of isolating them?"

"No." Firm and with a shake of the head. "They are very much Anthony's men. I can make no penetration at all."

Suffix pulled his notebook towards him and began to make detailed notes as he continued to question the General more closely about the Government Security Corps.

Ada answered the telephone with a long drawled "Yes?"

It is said that only those who have been reared in the snob class confines, or among serious debt, answer the telephone in this manner.

"Ada?" Boysie's voice came out in a furtive whisper.

"Mmmm." It meant the affirmative.

"Boysie."

"Well, hallo, Oaksie."

"Mummy and Daddy home?"

"Still abroad."

"What about Toby?"

"Still in Scotland. There's only cook, the daily woman and Fisher our aged retainer. Oh and me of course: there's always me."

"I've got to see you."

"How super. Alone at last?"

"Can I come over?"

"I'd rather you . . . Sorry, I was going to make an awfully vulgar joke. Come as you please, darling boy. I shall be waiting for you."

It was no time for austerity. Boysie took a cab to Richmond.

Ada opened the door wearing nothing but a smile and a towelling robe.

"Awfully good of you to make it so quickly, darling, come on up."

"I've got to talk to you. This is . . ."

"Up." Firmly she propelled him towards the stockbroker Tudor staircase.

"Look, Ada. We're all likely to be in . . ."

"Here, darling." Opening the door; dragging him into her bedroom all white and chintzy.

"Ada. I've got to . . ." Boysie protested.

"Pay your dues. Yes, Oaksie, sweetie. Sense my vibrations; they're good, clean and longing for you to pay up."

"Listen to me."

"After."

"I must . . ."

"Get undressed."

"Ada."

Her fingers clutched at his jacket. "Now listen, Ada. You remember when you joined the firm they said . . ." His jacket lay on the floor as she gently pushed Boysie into a sitting position on the end of the bed. ". . . They said there were prospects of travelling?"

She had his shoes and socks off and began to work on his shirt buttons; kissing his ear and the back of his neck.

"Well, the moment has come. You're being asked to travel, but I want you all to follow my lead . . ." Her mouth fastened on to his ear: tongue searching deep. "Ada, you're not listening."

"Come on, darling. The trousers."

Zip. Unbutton. Unbutton. Yank.

"Please, Ada. This is terribly . . ."

"Lift your bottom."

Jerk.

"I say, Oaksie. Continental for men, in super colours. Get your knickers off."

"Will you wait a minute. I have . . ."

"Always wanted to do this. Must be the Les in me."

Boysie felt his briefs give at the waist as she wrenched.

"Hey. You're . . ."

"Rippin' your drawers." Ada stood back to admire her handiwork. "Come on, then."

"Ada, for the last time."

"I've seen stronger looking things hanging in butchers' windows, darling. Let's see what I can do about it."

Ada tugged at the belt of her robe and let it fall to the floor. She was naked, young, tender, blossoming, etcetera.

"Rise, Sir Knight," said Ada. She smiled with pleasure. "That's more like it."

"Ada. I can't tell you howmmmmmm."

She stopped Boysie's mouth with her lips leaping towards him, on him, in him, or he in her, or . . . working. Tongues. Thighs. Sweat. Heavy. Breathing. Harder. Working harder. Together. Faster. Faster.

"Now what was it you wanted to tell me, love?" Ada came out of the shower still sprinkled with water. Little droplets dewing the smooth skin.

Boysie was lying where she had left him, taking gulps of air, on the bed, an ugly bite showing livid on his shoulder.

He recovered himself in a matter of minutes and carefully recounted the facts of Mostyn's peremptory orders.

"Actually that's awfully super." Ada, tall and almost skinny from some angles, stepped into her panties and pulled them tight, restraining her buttocks in a way which made Boysie wince. "I've always wanted to visit Africa."

"Hear me out."

"Sorry."

"I've been ordered to organise you all. But I rather hoped we could get a situation going whereby the three of you refused to act as hostesses."

"Not a chance. Why?"

"Ada, I can't go into details, but the whole thing's dangerous."

"Why didn't you tell Mostyn?"

"I think he knows. But Mostyn's . . . Well he's Mostyn."

She had her bra on by this time. "You don't like Mostyn do you, Oaksie?"

"No." He was trying to cover what was left of his manhood with the rumpled bed linen.

Ada sat on the bed, too close for any comfort. "You're frightened of him. Why? Come on. You can tell me."

Boysie felt a great retch of desire building. Desire to explain. To try and explain. "Some people have the power to intimidate," he said lamely. "They can somehow get under another person's skin. They seek out the weak areas and they have the necessary confidence. Mostyn knows he can intimidate me. Known it for years. Grief, there are plenty of people who have the trick. Husbands do it to wives; wives to husbands; nothing new about it." He paused. a ten-second break for thought. "Do you dislike him?"

"He's a foxy gentleman. Full of guile. But please, Oaksie, don't spoil our fun just to get your own back on Mostyn."

Boysie raised his eyes in supplication. "It's not a question of getting my own back. This is a serious business. It's liable to be very dangerous. Bloody dangerous."

"How dangerous?"

"I can't go into details but we're being used. Bloody dangerous, with real blood."

"I think we should take a vote. I shall ring round the others and ask them to lunch so that you can explain yourself fully. Then we'll take a vote. Democratic."

Boysie showered and dressed while Ada telephoned the other two girls.

"They're on their way," she announced. "So before they arrive we have a tiny job to do."

"Job?"

"Terribly simple actually." There was a pen in her hand, and a card. The card was exactly the same as the one Aida had made him sign.

"Look, what's going on?"

"Nothing's going on. It's just a memento sexualis. If you would sign the card, add the date and keep it safe."

"Yes. Well." Boysie took the card and looked at it. A

133

plain card with Ada's name typed in the corner. Identical to Aida's card. "I think I should know more. You're having me on, aren't you?"

Ada smiled sweetly. "We're having you, darling. Just a simple bet. You keep the card." She bent to kiss him. Being a gentleman at heart, Boysie did not pull away. The kiss developed, enlarged into mutual fumblings and gropings, expanded and involved the removal of certain garments, took the form of actions which spoke with a higher volume than whispers.

"For your age you're quite a virile beast," muttered Ada at the end.

"I just don't like being taken for granted."

Ada rearranged her clothing. "If you'll sign the card and date it then add the word 'twice'." She preened herself in the mirror.

Boysie did her bidding and tucked the card away in his wallet.

For lunch, served by the faithful Fisher, they had some kind of dark soup and a stew of what Boysie took to be veal, carrots and onions. The girls paid him much attention and appeared most excited about the possibility of the coming adventure. Boysie told them all that he dared: that the whole business was fraught with danger and that they would be much safer staying in London.

But they were young, throbbing women. The sniff of possible action passed up their nostrils and opened imaginations. In the end they flatly refused to strike.

"It's all very well," Boysie was like a mother hen. "But I'll be responsible for you. If we do go I want your solemn promises that you will do exactly what I tell you . . ."

"Any time," they chorused.

"You're shameless."

"Anything you tell us?" Aida looked up from under the big eyelashes.

"What happens if we disobey?" Alma's voice full of hope.

"We get bare bottom spankings, darlings." Ada squirming with pleasure at the thought.

"I do wish you would take this seriously," Boysie sighed.

"Oh, we do." They plumped their arms on the table and hunched forward in concentration.

They did, in fact, treat the matter more gravely when Boysie suggested that they should take the precaution of being armed.

"Those weapons Ada's folks have down in the cellar. One each. They'll fit in your shoulder bags."

"I'd be terrified carrying a gun around." Aida sounded as if she meant it, and it took Boysie the best part of ten minutes to convince them that it would be a wise move. In the end they agreed to carry the pistols, unloaded but with a full magazine separately in their shoulder bags.

They spent the rest of the afternoon in the cellar, Boysie attempting to instil the art of weapon handling.

They departed early in the evening and Boysie arrived at the Eaton Place flat a little after eight.

Snowflake Brightwater tapped her foot with the firmness of Buddy Rich, but the beat was augmented with irritation.

"And where have you been all day, Brian Oakes, child of my every waking thought and most of my dreams?"

"Business," Boysie muttered, surly, sexually spent from the morning's exertions with Ada, and suffering from a lean, mean streak of guilt. Why? Guilt on behalf of S. Brightwater, the oddball, screwball, elegant knickers-dropping, private and confidential quaint lady? Guilt because he had let the aristocratic, phoney-familied Ada screw him on her bed and had reciprocated and now could not raise the fare for Snowflake? Or guilt because the fear was starting to pressure, beginning to rise to danger point with the needles tripping over into that area marked in red where the black thoughts spun and ripped into one's gut and consciousness? Boysie realised that he had spent almost an entire day playing around with a trio of woolly-headed little birds who did not know about things like somebody having their head shot off while you just stood there, or people chasing you, and the sheer flimsy nightmare terror of real violence: the true stuff which included a great amount of pain and sweat. It was no time for guilt.

"I've been working and I'm bloody tired." He spat.

She closed the door. He got the impression of her nostrils flared and the arch of her beautiful eyebrows. Ché and John Lennon leered from their posters. "Screw you too," Boysie murmured.

"I tried your flat and the office. Every half-hour on the hour and the half-hour I've been calling you."

"I've been practising with my pistol."

"You gleam, dear heart; you gleam and glint in the eye. Pistol practice?"

"Yes. Bang-bang."

"I know how it goes." She poured two glasses of brandy. She poured them quickly, like someone intent on getting the stuff into their stomach fast and going on to something else. There was a sureness about all her actions.

Wasting time, Boysie thought. All day wasting time. If he had to be closely involved in the mechanics of this business then he should not have spent the day with the birds, especially arming them.

"I've got a report." He said it like a boxer squaring up.

"Bang-bang."

"You want to hear it and take it to the Marx Brothers?"

"Sweetest," Snowflake Brightwater raised her glass and tweaked her skirt so he did not know where to look. He was conscious of randiness sweeping him again like an alcohol rub. Christ, at my age, he thought. Three in a day is not bad. "Shoot." Snowflake's finger pointed like a gun. A pistol. The phallic symbol of virility and power. Balls.

"The flight Air Apparent has going with Excelsior on the tenth. On Wednesday."

"What of it?"

"I have to be on it. We are providing the cabin crew. The three girls and myself."

She began to laugh. He saw the pink interior of her mouth. The arched eyebrows. He ached for Miss Snowflake Brightwater. Yet in the middle of the ache there was something else. The laugh. His father's laugh on a good day when they talked of ships and the sea; of the places he had visited, now unrecognisable from the erosion of progress.

"Darling, it's so funny. You'll be serving me. Mr Frobisher

called. He wants me on that flight. That's why I've been trying to get you all day."

"That the only reason?"

"Of course not. I wanted . . ."

"Okay."

The brandy ignited his larynx and burned a smooth passage downwards. Boysie stood up and walked to her. Her face with the questioning look. Palms moist as he took hold of her, lifting her from the chair and leading towards the bedroom: their progress like a square dance. Honour your partners, he thought. Okay, I'll honour my partner.

He kicked the bedroom door shut with his heel and began to unbotton her shirt. Took her mouth on his. Slipped the shirt from her shoulders. She wore no bra and Boysie dropped his lips to her right nipple. Now the left. Erect and solid.

Button and zip of her skirt. Kicking his own shoes off and unzipping. Unbuttoning. Dropping. In one movement he peeled her pants off. Then her tights. Back onto the bed. Bare knees between hers forcing her legs open. Mouth to mouth. Going down. Penetrating.

"Boysie, I love rape. Let me know what it's . . ."

Three times in a day at his age was not bad until he remembered what someone had once told him about his anxiety spasms. At the edge of danger, in anxiety, he tended towards sensuality. At times like these he was not taking pleasure, giving pleasure, showing affection or love. He was attempting to return to the womb. He was escaping.

Later, much later, back in the Earl's Court Road flat, Boysie again felt the onset of the doubts, fears, nerves and desire to dig back into the past.

He went to the cupboard and took out the big mahogany box, spread out the second chart and, far into the night, re-enacted the Battle of the Nile.

11

ONCE YOU REACHED the main Otuka road, from the track which led through the forest, it was a straight drive into the capital. On the outskirts was Alaki Barracks: the old colonial barracks. Victorian and solid.

Suffix went through it all again in his mind, the plan on the table. His mercenaries, together with the men they had trained at the camp, would go straight to the barracks. General Bushway would be there with the troops loyal to him. They would drive in on the straight road which passed through Independence and Assembly Squares.

One detachment would move up Queen Elizabeth Street to take the radio and television station. A larger force had to carry on and occupy the House of Assembly and the Government Administration Building. If there was going to be trouble it would happen there. There was plenty of space in the Square of the Assembly and in the walled garden behind the House of Assembly. Detachment to the post office and a handful of men to the Hotel Europa, the city's largest hotel, which had a vantage overlook from its roof.

Suffix would peel off with Bushway and the best hundred men at the Square of Independence. A cordon round the president's house. Up the steps and in. That was the second tricky point. If one of the Government Security Corps men got happy with a trigger it might be unpleasant. The thought stimulated Suffix.

When that was completed he would personally lead the force out to the airport and secure things there. The Excelsior flight was due to make its unscheduled stop around ten in the morning. That was one thing he wanted tied up. There should be no problem. Unloading and refuelling, they knew from the previous experience, only took around one and a half hours. The weapons could go straight to the barracks. The aircraft could be airborne by noon. There were two flights in during the afternoon. None after six. Six in the evening was H-Hour for the coup.

He would make the airfield secure and do a tour of all sections and all roadblocks. The whole business should be over by nine. The only thing then would be the reaction of the remaining troops. If they threw in their hand with General Bushway there was no problem. If not? Suffix smiled. By dawn on the twelfth they would all know.

He leaned back, carelessly drumming his fingers. He thought of Bushway. The big black man. Government on behalf of the people, that was how the General had put it. Military control with labour enforcement leading to a strong economic development, instead of the soft, wheeling dealing diplomacy of President Anthony's regime.

To Suffix it made sense, even though he knew some would call it fascism.

On Monday morning Boysie called at the bank before going into the office. Once at the office he bought one of the flight tickets, paying for it with cash and inserting the name Charles Griffin on the booking list.

He went into his own office, addressed an envelope to Charles Griffin, marked it first class mail, sealed the ticket inside, then again left the building to post the letter.

It was not until that was completed did he do anything about buying Snowflake Brightwater's ticket with the cheque she had given him on the previous evening. He spent a long time trying to reason things out. If Frobisher, Pesterlicker and Colefax were going to stop the flight they seemed to be going about it in an odd way: getting their prize lady to buy a ticket.

Now, time did not allow him to figure it. Excelsior came through at noon to say they had arranged a one-day course, for Tuesday: so that the girls could become conversant with the aircraft, galley and foods.

At lunchtime Boysie gathered them together and said he was closing the office that evening. They only had three tickets left for the trip. Tomorrow the girls would be on the course. On Wednesday, he told them, they must sleep. The following twenty-four hours were going to be rough. They would meet again at eight o'clock on Wednesday night prior to doing the Victoria Coach Station circus. The flight was scheduled to leave Gatwick at eleven thirty.

President Anthony was almost seventy years old. He had seen many changes in Africa. He had also faced death before. He remained placid and unmoved by what the man told him.

The man who spoke was a white man. He was known to President Anthony and trusted by him. The president listened until he had finished.

"This does not surprise me." President Anthony's hands were on his lap, resting one across the other. "My own people have had suspicions. Even concrete facts. Are you sure of the timing?"

"Nobody can be sure. Except those who oppose you, President. But it seems right. The facts fit, if you follow me."

"And what course of action do you advise?"

"I can set certain things moving. Naturally we would like to see his threat dispersed with minimum trouble. My country would prefer to deal with it quietly."

The president nodded. He continued to nod as the white man talked of plot and counter plot.

Boysie called Griffin from his flat on Tuesday morning. "You get an airline ticket in the post this morning?"

"That Mr Oakes?"

"As I live and breathe."

"I got the ticket, but it's a bit short notice. I try to please, but . . ."

"Vital. Good pay. You said business was bad."

"Is this the matter we were discussing?"

"Partly. I simply want you covering me in the first instance."

"And in the last instance?"

"Another story."

"I'll have to hear it, Mr Oakes."

"Not on the blower. Can you come down to my place?"

Griffin sighed. "All right. Give me an hour."

"You won't regret it."

"Are you sure, Mr Oakes? Are you really one hundred per cent certain that I won't regret it?"

There was a click in the earpiece and Griffin was gone.

He arrived at the flat almost exactly one hour later.

"You see that?" asked Griffin, tapping a small item on the front page of the *Mail* which lay on the table.

The item concerned an unfortunate who had been fished out of the Thames near Waterloo Bridge.

"Very neat job that." Griffin looked pleased. "Nasty piece of work, that gent. And a nice, neat job. A testimonial if you like. Now, Mr Oakes, what's the breeze?"

Boysie told him all he knew. Griffin looked sad. "So you want me as a sort of hired gun?"

Boysie nodded.

"Don't like the thought of the three young birds tooled up. Guns can be very dodgy on an aeroplane as perhaps you know. Pop-Crunch-Suck-and-Wheeee, if you follow."

"Closely."

"Don't like that. Also, to be honest with you, Mr Oakes, I'm getting a bit old, a bit long in the tooth, to be capering about on this kind of fiddle."

A silence during which Boysie, blank-minded, counted from one to sixy-four.

"Shooters and pirate airlines and illegal arms distribution and putting the big wooden spoon into Africa. Doesn't sound like Mostyn." Griffin finally spoke as though to himself.

"It sounds like Mostyn," said Boysie. "Mostyn'd make a good gun runner. Run his guns up you any time."

"I don't care for it, Mr Oakes." Griffin gave a sigh like

a full stop; a definite point; a decision. "But as it's for you, I'll do it."

Boysie nodded. "Thanks. Incidentally, there's a bird as well."

"I might have known." Griffin did not smile. Birds and his kind of business did not go together.

"Are you allowed to share the secret of Frobisher Hall with me?" Boysie had taken the ticket over to Eaton Place and now sat on the bed while Snowflake Brightwater made decisions of moment concerning her wardrobe for the forthcoming trip. One large green Revelation Silverline was open, ready for packing, on the floor.

Snowflake allowed some goassamer creation to sink slowly onto the bed cover. "They only want me to take the ride to Africa and put in a report. I am there as an observer. I am the eyes of the outfit."

"You might like to know I've hired protection."

"After the other night I need protection, darling. Don't know what got into you."

The clouds came down again: the hum and whine of anxiety insinuating themselves into his mind, putting everything on a tilt. There was this minute spot in the centre of his being which told him that all was not well. The whine increased. It was as though the focus became more clear giving him almost a second sight. If someone had crept into the building and, now, had his hand on the door knob, Boysie would know. More, he could take action. The nerves reacted and there was an enormous sense of power. This was a transformation of his fears, as though all that had been soft and shaky was now turned into a new, hard brightness. It was a sense of advantage he must not jettison.

He said farewells to Snowflake. A long farewell that involved bodies and their intertwining. When he hit the street it was like coming from a sauna and massage.

Back at the flat, Boysie prepared himself a hot milk drink, stripped and performed ten minutes of strenuous exercise. The Diamondback was on his night table, loaded. Two tablets with the hot drink and an alarm call for five o'clock the following afternoon. Boysie climbed into bed.

The night noises of the Earl's Court Road filtered up from the street. Feet on the sparkling pavements, the rev of motors and the whoop of loud bucko boys tearing up the town.

There was spray in his face and Mostyn stood beside him. Mostyn wore a big black and gold cocked hat with the skull and crossed bones insignia embroidered large on the front. He also wore a medallion with a cobra spitting fire engraved upon it and carried a flintlock pistol.

There was carved wood. But they were flying and the spray came from the clouds which rolled by them like bucking seas.

When he woke it was eleven in the morning. Wednesday morning. The morning of Wednesday the tenth. Consciousness began to flood in. Boysie dammed the flow, covered his head and retreated into sleep again.

The troops moved fast and with skill. They were mixed, black and white, wearing jungle green combat suits. They worked with precision, making the obstacles look easy.

Colonel Peter Suffix, in his distinctive denim uniform, gun belt and the silver locket, watched the men as they cleared the final obstacle in the assault course, a barricade of logs and barbed wire.

Suffix nodded to Tilitson who stood beside him. "They look good. You're happy with discipline?"

"No problems, sir. They're your men. There is absolute obedience."

"That's what we must have." Suffix was not merely thinking about the tight-rope action in which they would be involved tomorrow evening. Suffix's mind travelled well ahead to the moment, two or three days hence, when he would be in total command of the army.

President Anthony smiled. The white man stood before him with a dozen members of the Government Security Corps: his most trusted men.

"You see," said President Anthony, "we have many friends. I understand that a large portion of the army has left the capital and are engaged in exercises in the north." He signalled to a pair of the GSC men, tall, young, solid looking with wide shoulders. "The troops on exercise are under the command of Colonel Impato. A good friend. At two o'clock tomorrow afternoon, no earlier, you will hand these personal instructions to Impato and then return here."

The president held out a thick envelope which was taken by the taller of the two GSC men.

Inside the envelope were orders that had been drafted by the white man. The orders were simple and explicit: they called for immediate action. All communications posts were to be manned immediately by men who were undoubtedly loyal to the president. This was to be followed by the arrest of certain officers and technicians, including the transport officers. The further orders called for cool calculation and speed.

The Girls all looked sharp and bright. They had taken the trouble to have their uniform scarlet tunics and flared pants pressed; each had been to the hairdresser, and the combined make-up would have done credit to the dolly svelte models of Monsieur Yves St Laurent.

Boysie had rejected the idea of being ultra geary. He wore one of his better dark suits, a Cardin, close-waisted with flared vents. He carried an airline overnight bag with spare shirt, underwear, and an Aramis Trip Kit. His peaked cap was on his head and the Diamondback, heavy and deadly, in his hip pocket. He looked like a man going places.

"Okay kids, let's go and sock it to 'em. All got your cutlasses and hook hands?"

"Sic transit gloria mundi," plummed Ada.

"Who dat?" Aida asked.

"Old Confucian proverb," explained Alma. "Means if your sick in transit don't worry because you'll be seeing Gloria on Monday."

"Ah so," they chorused, swinging out into the street.

"Will I do?" said Aida falling into step beside Boysie.

"For what?"

"For hostessing on a jet-plane?"

He took a long look. "It's right. Black is beautiful. Very beautiful and there's no justice."

"Why thank yo' Mistah Bow-sea. I shua take kindly to dem compliments."

The Victoria Coach Station scene was freaky. Boysie approached it in his usual manner and simply went through the actions, pretending it was not really happening. Faces young, old, indifferent, gnarled, worried, frightened, tired, amused, loomed up and around him. Squash and chatter. The eternal problems.

"You'll just have to wait for us, I'm afraid, my little girl has to use the toilet."

"If she wants a lavatory, madam, she must have one. All part of the Air Apparent service."

"She doesn't need a lavatory." The woman was thin and not to be trifled with. "She needs somewhere to be sick."

"A good start." Boysie felt the first tweaks of his own anti-flight obsession.

There were coats and hats, suitcases and handbags, parcels, umbrellas, warts, spectacles, magazines, trembling hands clutching at the rails of the coaches, dinky shoes, clumpy shoes and big cheap golden buckles. Boysie, having heaved what seemed like sixteen tons of baggage, stood back and watched Aida shepherding the clients aboard the big six-wheelers.

As he watched he was suddenly attacked by a monstrous hate for the crush, grab and bite of life in the teeming seventies. This is it, isn't it? Life lived to the frolicking full. The high-risers; the rising highs; the set-jetters who have overtaken the jet-set; everybody stand in line and wait your turn 'cause it's coming as sure as hell. Wait for the beautiful hamburgers pre-packed and swimming in tomato sauce that never saw a tomato let alone knew what one looked like. Or, lady, take the pre-taste-extracted beans, every nodule an explosion of flavour. Stand in line and we'll take you there on the limb of luxury: fruit cake, fortune cookies, whisky, gin, brandy, rum-flavoured wrist watches (or whatever happens to be in style) with six dials and a silver strap, baseball bats, credit cards, bank accounts, shops stuffed with people buying what they cannot afford and do not want while the other half starves (I gave my donation to Save The Children and Shelter), heady fabrics, soft next to the sweating skin oozing fragrance from bottles filled at twenty new pounds an ounce; stainless steel and silent pain-less porcelain cups. Oh what they would do for a bread roll and my magnificent mistress's left tit.

An illuminated hoarding across the road displayed a post office advertisement: a dolly bird, all slim thighs and black stockings, held a telephone to her ear, obscured by hair, her dress encrusted with numbers: *Remember* said the ad, *All-figure Numbers Now;* further down, the message wilted because they told you to ask the operator for *Freefone Service* 2013. "Ah, de numbers racket," spat Boysie, heading for the lead coach.

The transference of the passengers from their care to the tender mercies of the Excelsior ground hostesses was carried out with the minimum fuss.

Now they waited on the transit side of the building for the car to take them out to the aircraft ahead of the clients.

Boysie began to write his first novel in his mind. It started, *Gatwick shimmered in the light from twenty thousand kilowatts.* The plot became unsteady after that so he gave up. The girls chattered about the short course they had taken on Tuesday. Across the airport the roar of a Trident on take-off killed all speech.

The car arrived and dumped them near the forward gangway. There was activity and the throb of a dynamo. Boysie tried not to think about the actual experience of flight. He was faintly surprised to see how quickly the girls had learned. Once up the gangway they were nipping about making sure everything was neat for the arrival of passengers. Ada checked the loudspeaker system and turned on the tape.

Mantovani and his strings softly insinuated themselves into the main cabin.

Boysie took off his jacket and put on the white steward's coat hanging in the galley. From the flight deck he could hear the three crew members going through their pre-flight checks. He went forward and stood in the flight deck door. The captain stopped work and leaned back: a man of around fifty, bearded, bald and smooth.

"I'm Captain Morgan."

Boysie stifled the grin, nothing could be better than the bold bad pirate Henry Morgan.

"You'll be Mr Oakes from Air Apparent?" continued the captain.

"Acting unpaid steward."

"Well, just keep the coffee coming and the passengers out of our hair and we'll do fine. The first officer's name is Evans and that's Eric McKensie." He nodded towards the flight engineer who was checking things beyond Boysie's limited comprehension. "You know we do one scheduled unscheduled stop to refuel at Otuka?"

Boysie inclined his head.

"We've got a spare crew there as well. Use it as a slip station. Okay?" The captain turned back to the frenzy of instruments. "You can let 'em on as soon as they arrive."

Within ten minutes Boysie and Ada were standing at the top of the gangway as the great straggle of passengers disgorged themselves from the coaches below.

Among the first to board was Snowflake Brightwater, wearing the black velvet pants suit, leather coat and wide hat she had worn at her first meeting with Boysie.

Snowflake paused at the top of the stairs and shook out a tiny smile at Boysie. "I have come to enter belly of great winged silver bird," she said.

"And great winged silver bird welcomes you," Boysie replied.

A few seconds later, Griffin plodded aboard with a swift nod.

Still they came. The cabin began to fill. Then, Boysie glanced down to see how many clients remained. His eyes widened. Mounting the gangway were five black gentlemen, each clothed in identical dark blue suits, wearing bowler hats and carrying Samsonite briefcases. It was Mister Colefax and his muscle men.

"W-we s-sit at the b-b-b-back," said Mister Colefax without explanation.

Snowflake Brightwater, Griffin and the Colefax Boys. It was a good title for a movie, thought Boysie as his gut began to churn in apprehension.

12

THE FOOL'S RIM of terror. The apocalyptic moment of anxiety. There had been a time when, even to Boysie, this particular fear, seen in retrospect, contained humour. Not any more.

He tried to be logical, stimulating the brain to accept facts: that once you had a certain aerodynamic shape, a definite amount of power producing a particular thrust, at a given moment the shape would take to the air and fly: a scientific proof as obvious as rain, hail and all the natural elements.

But, for Boysie, none of these things mattered. Science could go stick its polluted butt into some of its own manu- factured fertiliser. When the power built up, making the aircraft strain and shake like a giant in labour: when the brakes came off and she began that long run into the sky, the bluest funk, starkest terror, heart-thumping, nerve-strangling anxiety took over. It was not funny and he could do nothing about it.

They seemed to have been roaring down the runway for ever. Then the smoother sensation, followed by a slight drop and tilt. Thump and the landing gear retracted, locking away.

On the flight deck it had been a normal routine take-off with no problems. The First Officer called London radar and was given his clearance out. As he started the after-takeoff checks they climbed through cloud to an operational height of twenty-five thousand feet, turning onto airway Amber Two which would take them across Europe down through Italy. The first leg. The flight crew unbuckled their seat belts.

In the cabin, the *No Smoking: Fasten Seat Belts* sign flicked off. Boysie, skin still singing from shock, reached for his cigarettes with relief, then realised that he had work to do. Ada had already gone past him to the loudspeaker system while Alma and Aida took up positions in the main aisle, each holding a life jacket.

Boysie moved forward as Ada began her spiel about safety. The other two girls pointed out the emergency exits; they demonstrated the oxygen masks that would drop in the event of depressurisation and told the passengers how to hold them over their faces. They said nothing about how quickly lack of oxygen hits you, or of the split second you needed to get one of those masks onto your face in such an emergency.

Boysie standing behind Ada, watched as she read the printed form as though she had been doing it for a thousand years. She was a natural, he thought, what with that posh voice she managed to downgrade for this kind of activity.

Ada got to the bit about the lifejackets being under the seats and how you had to put them on and how you must not inflate them inside the aircraft and the flashing light and whistle and all. Alma and Aida were going through the motions all the time, putting on the life jackets and showing people where the little whistle and flashing light were. They did it with poise, yet differently from airline hostesses Boysie had seen in the past. It was not until they reached the end of the demonstration that he realised what the difference was. These girls were making it sexy. They could have been strippers in a first rate joint like the Crazy Horse or that place he had been told about where they shed their threads on parallel bars.

"Okay, Oaksie." Ada finished the safety lecture. "Let's get the show on the clouds. One drink the Excelsior man said, then shoot the dinner to them. Don't encourage any more drinking and get the dinners on quick so they'll sleep."

Alma and Aida joined in.

"That looks real good." Aida rolled her eyes. "Lady in Row K: Seat Five. Very pregnant and could well have it in flight."

The terrors of takeoff vanished. There were problems here that Boysie had never dreamed about.

The flight deck door opened the flight engineer leaned out. "Where the bloody hell's the coffee? How do you expect us to keep this thing going without coffee?"

Ada motioned the other two to start taking orders while she dealt with the crew. Boysie, already deciding his rôle should be the same as Snowflake Brightwater's—that of an observer—slowly began to walk towards the back of the aircraft.

Mr Colefax and his cronies sat smiling in tandem pairs, Colefax himself sitting apart from the heavies in one of the triple rows, on the outer seat.

Boysie grinned at Colefax who grinned back and raised a hand. The first and second fingers were crossed in a significant gesture.

Boysie turned and looked down the length of the cabin. Rows of heads, constant movement, the girls going about their business of providing liquid refreshment. The fact of flying insinuated itself into his mind for a second, then the brain squall. Colefax's men were most certainly armed. Five weapons. He had the Diamondback. Six. Griffin. Seven. Each of the girls. Ten. Snowflake Brightwater? Doubtful. Ten weapons in the close confines of the cabin. Below the cabin was the baggage. Captain Morgan had told him that they were making the stop at Otuka which looked like the usual fiddle. They were almost certainly carrying a prize cargo. Rifles for the revolutionaries. Machine guns for the agitators. Automatic pistols for anarchists. So watch the wall my darling while the gentlemen in the streamlined, stratospheric flying Boeing 707 go by. Har-har, Jim. You could be a pirate in Hackney Wick or Haiti: a smuggler man at Dover, Delhi or Des Moines, Iowa. You did not need a galleon or much brain. Just essential contacts and, like Mostyn, you could pirate the airways and carry carnage to any part of the world. It was at this moment that Boysie, in spite of Colefax, Snowflake and anybody else, decided that some specific and direct action should be taken. Fate had placed him on board so fate would have her way. Oakes would see that this particular consignment of death would not get through. The people who had sent Mostyn to do their shopping would be upset. Uptight upset. Mostyn would inevitably be upended. The other matter swam into view. The far back matter of his father. There would be time for that. If necessary he would squeeze it from Mostyn like squeezing the life from a chicken . . .

Boysie began to trundle back down the aircraft's aisle.

Part way down, Griffin's hand rose and tugged at him. "Large whisky and soda, steward," Griffin said loudly. Then, in a hiss, "Your shooter's showing through that uniform jacket, Mr Oakes."

Boysie's hand went automatically to his hip pocket. He nodded thanks and hopped forward, clutching his rear like a man recently the recipient of a painful injection.

The forward loo was empty. Inside he altered the position of his weapon, shifting it to the unhealthy right hand trousers pocket. More people, he thought, get their balls blown off this way. It was most uncomfortable and could also give the wrong impression to the girls if he happened to bump into them accidentally. Lethal that would be, he mused. A high powered ejaculation. Still, the eggheads reckoned pistols were power symbols, sexual in origin. He did not see it himself, but if all the brainy blokes came up with it that way, it must be right.

The girls were doing feats of acrobatic juggling with trays and glasses.

"Good party?" smiled Boysie as Aida squeezed by hell bent on delivering alcohol to the customers.

"I just pray we don't get raided," she snarled. "There are two kids freaking out on pot in Row H; our pregnant lady looks unwell; I've spotted a pair of possible heart cases and a young man in Row C is groping the girl next to him."

"Does she object?"

"No. But there's a nun sitting next to her."

A cold wash over the nervous system. Someone had once told him that nuns on aeroplanes were considered very bad medicine.

Boysie gave a hand with the frenzy of serving dinner. A standard plastic tray complete with plastic chicken, salad, roll butter, fruit jelly, cheese and biscuits.

Aida looked at the first consignment sadly. "Looks delicious."

"No more than they deserve," Alma snapped. "Plastic food for plastic people, because that's what that lot are."

They served dinner. They served coffee. They served dinner and coffee to the crew. When all that was over, Captain Morgan came on the intercom system and introduced himself to the passengers like a disc jockey. He told them where they were and continued, "We will carry on at the present height for the remainder of the trip. In half an hour we pass over Rome where we follow the airways route across the Mediterranean, over Sicily and up over Libya, across Chad and Cameroon. We then follow the West Coast down to Luanda where we should arrive around eleven thirty tomorrow morning. I think you should all get some sleep now and I'll speak to you again at breakfast time."

Lies, all lies. Anyone on board who knew anything about anything could tell. They had to put in somewhere. In the galley, the light came on from the flight deck. Boysie went forward.

"You get breakfast over by nine," said Morgan. It was an order. "I give them the old story about having to put in to Otuka, as soon as I have clearance from there which should be about nine fifteen. We ought to be down, engines off, by nine thirty."

"Better be." The Flight Engineer looked up from his calculations. "Otherwise the engines'll stop by themselves."

Boysie went back, checked his personal liabilities—Colefax, Griffin and Snowflake. Snowflake was already asleep. The others looked happy.

He joined the girls in the galley and told them all that it was necessary for them to know about the landing at Otuka.

"I'm going to get some rest now," he said. "But make sure I'm awake by six. We serve breakfast at seven and by that time I should have come up with something. Just remember, it's our job to stop this stuff going into Otuka."

He stretched himself out on the long bench seat in the rest area, closed his eyes and thought about sleep and what had to be done.

The jets grumbled. It might have been a super train they were riding, on invisible rails. The Knightsbridge office came into focus. Far away as though it did not exist. The flat off Chesham Place from which he operated in the old days. Griffin on a pebble beach. The smooth life. Soft. Bloody soft nostalgia with music by people who had changed and moved on. What was it the Man said? You learned certain things by living. You learned that there was life and death. That was all. They did not tell you the rules. They tossed you in and you moved, and the first time you put a foot wrong they shot at you: more than often they killed you. So the trick of living was to accept the big trick of dying: a way to face it. Grace under pressure. That's what the Man called it. Had Lieutenant Robert Oakes shown grace under pressure? Had his son?

The growl of engines as they felt their way through the skies. It was a half-dream. Conscious unconsciousness. Taxis and buses. The pretty windows of Knightsbridge and a guitar tune by Villa-Lobos that kept back-tracking through his head. Head. Computer. Technology. Pollution. Corruption. With bodies making love? No, with bodies making power. Lust did not just have to do with sex; nor jealousy. Green as the something or other and deep as death. Rupert was liquid nostalgia, not just soft. Open the door onto the flight deck, draw out the gun and pull the plug on them. Mad? Okay, but little vomit drip Mostyn was not going to have things all his own way. Ada was shaking his shoulder and it was six o'clock.

Tilitson woke Suffix at six, his normal time. He stayed there on his back looking up at the rough wooden slats of the roof. It was his day. General Bushway's day.

Outside the men were already drilling. Physical training each morning before breakfast was the usual way the day began. It was like that for Suffix as well. He got out of bed and went through his pattern of exercises.

He felt good. Alive. Alert. Suffix knew that confidence in oneself, and those under your command, was, literally, half the battle.

Suffix went to shower. God knew when he would get an opportunity to shower again.

They finished serving and clearing breakfast by eight thirty. People were forming queues at both the loos: cleaning themselves up after the night. The captain spoke to the passengers during breakfast, saying that they had been given permission to reduce height as they flew down the coast, that the weather was good and there would be plenty to see on the way to Luanda.

Boysie crowded into the galley with the girls.

"Okay. This'll be quite straightforward and nobody's going to get hurt. I want you to be certain of what is going to happen. Around nine fifteen the Skipper'll give out his phoney message saying we have to land at Otuka. The story is that we'll only have enough fuel left to get in. When he cuts the chat I'll walk on to the flight deck and try to persuade them to go into another airport outside Etszika."

"What do you mean, persuade?" from Alma.

"I shall point a gun at them and threaten to blow holes in their instrument panel."

"Boysie, you can't." Aida excited, letting the cool blow a fraction.

"Stow it."

"But there're women and children on board."

"You don't think I know it. We're sitting on a flying time bomb anyway. I wouldn't dare use it. But a gun is powerful. Pilots do not dare take risks."

"What if he won't go to another airport?" Ada was chalky complexioned.

"Then I stay with them. I tell them that I start shooting: the flight engineer first and all that tough kind of Bogey jazz, if they horse around. Nothing to be moved off the aircraft. Just a straight refuel and off."

"What are we to do?" Ada again.

"Have your shoulder bags at the ready and the pistols unloaded. I want Alma at the rear of the aircraft. Aida halfway down and Ada here in the galley where she can

155

see the flight deck door. You stop people running interference."

"Anybody?" Aida looked coy.

"What're you getting at?"

"I just happened to notice little honeypot was aboard."

"Honeypot?" He knew it did not sound convincing.

"The honeypot you've been dipping into." Alma joined in.

"Yes. I noticed her." It was Ada's turn. "Miss Gatwick Takeoff 1970. Dig?"

"Oh, her."

"Do we stop her? Or is she part of the great aircraft robbery?"

"No." Boysie had the grace to look sheepish. "No, you needn't stop her, nor Mr Griffin. Row M: Seat one. He's on our side if it comes to a sort out."

"Are you certain this is for the honour of the country and the freedom of mankind and all the rest?" Ada's voice had the feel of a gimlet: the kind you did not drink.

"What are you . . .?"

"You seem to have things pretty well sewn up that's all."

"Love, it's a heavy operation. Trust me . . ."

He was about to go into his big finish with all the arguments about really keeping the peace and stopping the greedy little men from making a pile of gold on the bodies of their brothers, but without any warning the engine note changed from its steady throb and they yawed drastically.

The lurch threw them together against the forward bulkhead. The engine noise on the starboard side had undoubtedly deteriorated: everything had a different feel about it—the aircraft's attitude; the power. Instead of a pulsing rumble there were a series of grumbles, and the machine itself strained against the air instead of riding it. These were things you could sense with your feet and in the growing dot of anxiety at the centre of your brain.

Very slowly the situation resolved itself, returning to a normality that was not the normality of five or ten minutes before. Boysie physically jumped as the loudspeaker system clicked on.

"That's friend Morgan." He looked at his watch. It showed nine ten. "Get to your places and stop anyone following in."

Morgan began talking. As he did so, Boysie noticed the steward's call light, from the flight deck, was glowing.

"This is the captain speaking. There is no cause for concern, but we have a slight emergency. A little trouble with an engine which we have shut down. The aircraft will operate quite efficiently on three engines and we have already called Otuka airport for clearance to land there. If you will stay in your seats, fasten seat belts and extinguish cigarettes we will be landing at Otuka within the next few minutes. I will try to make the delay as short as possible."

Alma and Aida were off up the cabin.

Boysie was impressed by the captain. His chat was convincing. Boysie could tell that by the way his hand shook on the flight deck door handle.

He opened the door and stepped onto the flight deck. Everybody seemed to be working hard and there was a lot of sweat around.

The vibrations were not good, but there was no point in turning back now. Boysie's hand went into his pocket. It was a classic fumble: around seven seconds before he got the Diamondback out.

"All right." He found himself shouting. "Where's your nearest alternate? You're not going into Otuka."

The first officer half turned. The flight engineer's face, heavy with perspiration to his right, did not alter.

"Change your course and get to your nearest alternate or I blast out the instrument panel."

"He's not joking, Skipper." Inanely from the first officer.

"You must be joking, chum," Morgan roared, concentrating on the controls. "We're five miles from the Otuka threshold and it's all for real. The starboard inner's overheated so badly that it almost went up. My port inner's begun to overheat and I'm flying asymmetric. Apart from that we don't have an alternate. Blast away, I've no option."

"But . . ." struggled Boysie. His eyes lifted. They were

flying at around two thousand feet and you could feel the constant loss of height. Ahead, the coastline was bathed in a light rain mist. Foam on rocks and dirty sand. Dark olive green clusters.

"Gear down," said Morgan, taking no notice of Boysie.

The first officer moved. A few second later there was a distinct thump from the nose.

"Gear down three greens. No reds." The first officer sat eyes front.

"Excuse me." The flight engineer squeezed past Boysie.

They were lower now and you could make out the spread of a small city as it reached back from the seaboard: a scatter of buildings, white against the green and grey. To the immediate front the tiny stretch of dark runway.

"The suspense is killing me," yelled Morgan. "Are you going to blast us out of the sky?"

"You just get us down. We'll worry about the other bit when we're on the ground." The words tumbled over each other.

The first officer was talking away into his headset. "Alpha-Juliet-Bravo-Echo. Outer marker." Pause. "Bravo Echo."

"Spoilers in. Three-quarter flaps." From Morgan, repeated by the first officer.

"Brakes pressure zero."

"Brakes pressure zero."

"Nose wheel central."

"Nose wheel central."

The runway slid into line ahead. They dropped lower. Boysie felt his ears singing.

"You ready to cancel that engine, Eric?"

The Flight Engineer grunted, hunched over the console which ran between the captain's and first officer's seats.

"Call out my speeds, would you, she's a bitch to keep straight." Morgan was applying a good deal of physical exertion on the controls.

The first officer's voice maintained a quiet pitch. Underneath you could feel the tension.

"Seven hundred plus twelve . . . Six hundred plus thirteen . . ."

The engine roar settling to a whine and the ground coming up very fast below them.

"Five hundred plus twelve . . . Inner Marker . . ."

Boysie saw the end of the runway leaping out of what seemed to be scrub-strewn sand. They were very low over the sand as though they would chew into it at any moment. Morgan cursed and the nose yawed over to the right then back again.

"Four hundred plus eleven . . ."

Still riding just above the sand.

"Three hundred plus twelve . . ."

The end of the runway slid below them.

"Threshold . . ."

"Flare . . ." yelled Morgan.

The whole weight juddered as the main wheels struck the concerete, lifted, and struck again.

The nose came down with a bump. They were streaking fast, burning up runway.

"Cancel port inner. Full reverse both outers."

The engine note changed as the flight engineer's hands moved across the throttles like an organist doing a difficult bit of Bach.

The banshee howl of jets in reverse.

"Just pray the brakes hold." Morgan still shouting.

"Eighty knots . . ." From the first officer.

They were humping, rumbling, juddering more or less in a straight line, still eating up concrete.

"Seventy . . . Seventy-five . . ."

The far end of the runway was coming up. Lights. Wire. Scrub. Sand. Trees a couple of hundred yards on.

Slowing. A marked slowing.

"Cancel reverse."

The noise dipped to a low whistle.

Slow. Slowing to a halt.

The sound of breath being let out in long low sighs of relief.

Morgan turned from the controls. The aircraft was at a standstill. There was about fifty yards of runway left. "Okay, you'd better get on with your hijacking. You have a gun. What do you want us to do?"

"Get the refuelling done and take off for Luanda."

Morgan smiled. "Again you must be joking. Or weren't you with us through all that? We came in on two and a half engines."

"Can they be fixed without disembarking?"

"At a conservative estimate," Morgan stroked his beard, "I'd say that we will be lucky to get out of Otuka for twenty-four or forty-eight hours. We've really got problems, chum."

"Nobody leaves this aircraft." Boysie vainly attempted to sort out the patterns and pictures jumbled in his mind. "Nothing is to be unloaded and nobody leaves."

He had not heard the door open behind him.

"W-rong," stammered Colefax. Hard metal jabbed painfully into Boysie's right side. "Th-this is w-where w-we g-get off. I-I thought y-you w-were on our s-side, m-man."

13

Boysie HELD HIS breath and ground his teeth. Colefax had got past Ada and the situation was even more confused. He looked out of the right hand window. A truck pulling up on the runway: yellow, stationing itself in front of the aircraft.

"We're supposed to taxi in after that truck." Morgan sounded the least disconcerted.

"F-f-follow him th-then."

"No." From behind Colefax, Ada's voice. She had finally caught on.

There was a moment's pause and Boysie heard somebody else. "Terribly sorry but it's imperative that Mr Colefax gets off here." Slinky Snowflake Brightwater *had* been carrying a weapon. Now she had it on Ada.

"Let's have none of the old moody, darling. Drop it." A chain reaction had built up behind, Griffin now joining in.

Boysie stepped to one side avoiding Colefax's gun, a nasty looking snub-nosed automatic, originating from a Latin American country by the look of it.

Through the door, Boysie could see to the rear of the aircraft. Aida held down Colefax's men, very steady with the Llama VIII, and Alma was doing her best to look businesslike in the centre of the aisle.

The situation around the flight deck door had deteriorated to complete farce. Colefax was bugging his eyes at his gun, not knowing what to do next. Ada, who appeared to be very frightened, had the Standard Olympic pressed into Colefax's back. Behind her, Snowflake Brightwater, looking like a dude gunfighter from a smooth modern western movie. Butch Brightwater. The Sundance Kid stood behind her in the shape of Griffin, only he had that nervous professional look: like a constant window shopper round the porn boutiques.

In the main cabin the passengers seemed restless, worried and uncertain. Some were talking loudly, but the amount of hardware about was keeping them from action.

"Okay," Boysie desperately fought for time. "Follow him round, Captain. But nothing must be unloaded. You know what kind of cargo you're carrying?"

"We've got some farming implements to be dropped off here." He meant it.

Boysie nodded. "Nice farming implements. Ploughshares with a high rate of fire, and some charming muck spreaders that'd spread all of us into the ground."

"H-hey m-man, hon-hon-honestly it w-would b-be b-b-better t-to let things pr-r-roceed. It's all b-been t-taken c-care of, I p-promise." Colefax looked at him with eyes registering faith, hope and charity. "F-for the b-best."

"I think he's right, love." Snowflake turned her head towards him. "I don't know it all but we should arrive here as normally as possible."

"I don't know what . . ."

"Can I follow that truck without getting my chump blown off?" asked Morgan irritated by the situation.

"Go ahead. Yes," shouted Boysie as though he was washing his hands of the whole business. "You absolutely certain, Snowflake?"

She nodded. "Pretty positive. Mr Colefax is on our team, sweetie. He's anti the same people as you."

Boysie tried to use logic. They were at a foreign airport with an aircraft full of people and weapons. The captain seemed straight. Colefax had proved himself in London. Snowflake could prove herself anywhere. The circle of logic came back to himself every time. He had initiated the hijacking and the whole thing had fallen apart in his hands.

The two outer engines were grumbling and they began to move, slowly turning to follow the yellow truck.

Boysie looked at the flight engineer. "You really have got two engines U/S?"

"One definite. The other probable. We weren't playing games on that landing. It was bloody dodgy."

The facts began to weigh heavily on Boysie. It had been a badly timed and irresponsible action.

"How do I stand if I call my people off?" He looked at Colefax.

"It'll b-be okay."

"Can you square them?" He indicated the crew with a nod of the head.

"I got pa-papers, m-man."

"I was only doing what I thought best. Okay, show the man your papers and talk. Would the rest of you put away your firearms and go back to your places."

It was a dreadful anti-climax. Boysie, looking crestfallen, shuffled to the cabin loudspeaker control by the galley bulkhead, switched it to speak, and picked up the telephone-like instrument.

"This is the Chief Steward speaking—" he still hoped his decision was right—"we apologise for the delay and the anxiety you have been caused. We have landed at Otuka and at one time it was thought that we were victims of an attempted hijacking. The captain will speak to you shortly."

There was an odd sense of relaxed tension. The guns had disappeared. Alma and Aida were returning to the galley.

Boysie went back onto the flight deck. The first officer was taxiing the aircraft and the airport buildings were visible ahead. Colefax stuffed a wodge of papers back into his jacket pocket, grinned, nodded at Boysie and left.

"We won't monkey about with the kind of authority that one's carrying." Morgan looked grave. "He's vouched for you as well. Now I have to get on to the Company and fix hotels for everybody."

"I've told the passengers you'll speak to them."

"After I've talked with ground control."

Boysie went back into the cabin. Everybody seemed to be avoiding his eye so he went to Snowflake Brightwater for comfort.

"That was not a bright action." Miss Snowflake Brightwater kept her eyes rigidly to the front. "We are not amused. Somebody could have been killed."

"That's good coming from you. You were up there sharpish toting a gun."

"I was merely looking after the interests of Mr Colefax, as I was bidden. Mr Colefax's interests, as you will soon find out, are your interests."

The messenger arrived at the camp a little before one thirty and went straight to Suffix.

"The General gave me the message verbally. I have to report to you only."

Suffix had been resting. He sat on the bed, rubbing his eyes. A rest period had been ordered for everyone not doing essential duties.

"Well?"

"The aircraft arrived on time and the weapons have been unloaded and taken to the barracks."

"Good."

"No, there is more. There was nearly an accident. Trouble with two of the aircraft's engines. They nearly did not make it. The aircraft is grounded at Otuka and passengers and crew are staying at the Hotel Europa. The company is flying out spare parts."

"How many?"

"Spare parts?"

"Passengers."

"At least two hundred."

Suffix frowned. "When can they leave? How soon?"

"The General says not for two days earliest. That is what he hears."

Suffix stood up and crossed to his table and the detailed plan of Otuka. After several minutes he dismissed the messenger with instructions to tell the General that all would proceed as planned, the fact of an unexpected influx of visitors at the Hotel Europa would be noted. Then he called Tilitson.

"The hotel will be full. We'd reckoned on it being empty," Tilitson commented after hearing the news.

"Two hundred Europeans and South Africans in the city at this time. It's not good, but I want you to double the detachment we had already chosen to take the hotel. They are to be cautioned. There is to be no funny business with the guests. Nobody is to take liberties, Tilitson. I want those people out of here and back on their flight as quickly as possible. And I don't want them taking unpleasant stories out with them."

At two o'clock the pair of GSC men walked into the forest clearing where Colonel Impato, in command of the remaining Etszikan troops, had his field HQ.

They delivered President Anthony's sealed letter to the Colonel who read it twice before taking swift action.

"Something always happens, doesn't it, Mr Oakes?" Griffin sat in a cane chair next to Boysie. On the other side, Snowflake Brightwater stretched out her long and bedazzling legs. They were together on Boysie's balcony at the Hotel Europa following a lunch which had verged on being European and one star.

"Always," agreed Boysie, close wrapped in thought as he looked out across the street to where the South Atlantic washed onto a deserted and scruffy beach. It was hot and humid with clouds threatening more rain. Already, during the frenzied hours of organising transport and hotel accommodation, there had been two heavy storms.

"Tell it to me again." Boysie turned to Snowflake Brightwater who looked least crumpled of all.

"Tell what?"

"All you know."

"Mr Frobisher instructed me to travel on the aircraft and observe what happened. He also said that it was imperative Mr Colefax and his men disembarked at Otuka and that there was no interference with the normal running of the flight." She said it all in one breath, parrot fashion, then added. "I don't think he took possible engine trouble into account."

"Very touchy area, this," commented Griffin. "Never really operated here."

Boysie ignored him. "Did anyone notice what happened to Mr Colefax and his friends after we went through customs and immigration?"

"Vanished like a magician's ball."

"Into space."

"Well, they aren't in the hotel. Leastways not under their own names."

The hotel itself was solid and Victorian, like most of the larger buildings in Otuka, with the exception of the high-rise Government Admin Office and the modern House of Assembly. You could almost have been in a Northern railway hotel: apart from the fans, climate and service.

"Very touchy area," Griffin continued his monologue. "Got the smell of unrest. You can sniff it."

"That's probably the plumbing."

Boysie began to wonder if he was suffering from delayed shock. The edges of his being seemed frayed, and even the smallest action had begun to call for great concentration. For instance, it had taken him a solid ten minutes to make himself pick up the telephone and call room service for much needed drinks. That was a good half hour ago; room service had not yet appeared with the beverages.

Hot, sweaty and thirsty. Boysie ticked off these bodily conditions on his fingers and then turned his attention inwards to his mind. Uncalled, the scene on the flight deck during the landing returned, and with it a sliver of fear. At the time all fear had been concentrated in watching what was happening in a partial sense of disbelief. Only now did the full impact of near disaster make itself apparent. There was something else. He felt what Griffin felt: the scent of danger.

From behind them, in the room, came a loud knocking.

"The bloody drinks at last." Boysie prised himself from his chair and ambled to the door recognising fatigue in the stiffness of his bones.

"At last," said Mostyn, cool in a blue linen suit. "What in the name of blessed Saint Bona, patron of air hostesses, have you been at?"

"Oh Christ," said Boysie with feeling.

Mostyn carried an automatic pistol and behind him, smiling cheerfully, was one of Mr Colefax's team.

Colonel Impato reported in person to President Anthony. They met in the study at the president's residence. The president showed little sign of the strain that, by now, must have been taking hold. He sat at his desk, looking a good deal younger than his age, smiling greetings at the Colonel.

"All is being done." The Colonel took the chair indicated to him.

"You don't think Bushway's spies . . .?"

"They will not have had the time or opportunity. The General has never carried the bulk of our officers with him. I have a dozen people under arrest, no more. One can see why he has found it necessary to bring in mercenaries and malcontents from overseas. When they move we will act against them. Quickly and ruthlessly."

"I wish to stress that I desire minimum bloodshed."

"There is no need. We will do all that is possible to avoid combat. The police, incidentally, have been given their instructions. You need have no fears there. But there is one point. Your personal safety concerns me."

The president smiled again, a secret humour lighting his face. "Colonel Impato, members of my family have been leaders for a very long time. African leaders. Chieftains; Tribal Heads; now, even a president. We adapt; we change. We face the danger of our appointed position. We also have a clear view of the shifting span of history. I really believe we see much more in retrospect than even the esteemed Europeans. It is because we have lived with the threat of uprising and change, within our families, for centuries. We truly understand our own people."

"The Europeans have had their fair share of historical intrigue."

"But the mind is different." Almost whispered. "The mind and the ground, the country. I can smell my enemy. I know him too well."

"Bushway is dangerous. Do not underestimate him, Mister President."

"Any man who dreams of self-aggrandisement to the tune of upsetting a peaceful, growing community, is dangerous. Criminally so. But you must smell Bushway, the animal, to know him. I have known him for many years. He has a fair brain, but he is no soldier. We sent him to England for training before he became Commander of the Army, but I think I saw, even then, where his true goal lay."

The president paused, picking up a paper on his desk and dropping it back in place before continuing. "Bushway has dreams. He sees an ideal community here with himself at the head: yet it is a power complex in a man unable to control power. A more subtle man would have waited, but Bushway is impatient. Hence the mercenaries. You will see. When the moment comes he will hesitate for that second, like the gorilla who puffs himself up and beats his chest, wasting time before the attack. If we allowed this coup to proceed it would mean the collapse of the country."

"You are right, of course, that is why I am still concerned for your personal safety."

"I am well cared for. You look after the tasks that have been given you. Provide the men. The rest will be arranged. We have most excellent advisers."

"You must be sly, slimy little Mostyn." Snowflake Brightwater advanced towards the group at the door, cool as Françoise Hardy. The only noise came from the big clanking fan whirring from the ceiling.

Mostyn and the African came into the room. The African kicked the door closed behind him. Griffin stood between the balcony windows, one hand in his jacket, Napoleon style.

"Sly, slimy and little? Who would refer to me in those terms?"

Snowflake Brightwater nodded towards Boysie. "That's what he calls you."

Mostyn grunted. "Sit down. All of you sit down. I hear there's been stupidity."

Again it was the Mostyn of Boysie's nightmare: the man capable of intimidating, browbeating, barking, surrounded

168

by an invisible shield of breeding capable of putting men like Boysie at an immediate disadvantage.

"You shit." Boysie could think of no better description.

"Have care. I thought we'd taught you a few things. Now I hear you had a private army on that aircraft."

"I merely wanted to stop the run into Otuka."

Mostyn laughed: a short, unpleasant bray. "The run? You wanted to stop the run. Why?"

"Because shits like you shouldn't be allowed to get away with it."

Snowflake Brightwater and Griffin sat uneasily on the bed. Boysie had sunk into one of the two easy chairs: Mostyn had the other. The African leaned against the door. The oppressive heat built in the room like a thunderhead.

"So you play ducks and drakes with an aircraft full of people because you don't happen to like the way I operate."

"Not when you organise arms shipments to an explosive area like this. To make money. I know it's bloody old fashioned for people of my generation to question how others line their bank accounts. But I wouldn't be seen spitting into the same cesspool with you, Mostyn, and don't come the old 'if I didn't do it someone else would'."

"You learn nothing." Mostyn spoke quietly, "I try and spell it out to you because we've always worked on the need to know principle. Also it was necessary that you were only frontally involved in London. I spelled it out and you still didn't catch on. Oakes, you're a dolt and a buffoon and I really should never use you. How long have you known me?"

"Too long."

"Cut the *Boys' Own Paper* heroics. Do you really think I'm capable of . . .?"

Boysie did not let him finish. "Yes, I do, Mostyn. I bloody do. Your trouble is that you're bloody sneaky. You intrigue over the bodies of others. You've always done it. You always will. It's a trait of your class."

"Class?" Calmly.

The queried word stopped Boysie. "Oh, what the hell."

"Perhaps," hissed Mostyn, "it is a question of upbringing.

Breeding. The ruthless streak is also the streak of loyalty. Where are your women?"

"The girls?"

"Who else?" He sounded tired of argument; of even bothering to explain detail.

"They have a room on the fifth floor."

"Number?"

"Five twenty."

Mostyn's head gave a quick judder. He rose and crossed the room to the telephone by the bed. Picking up the instrument he asked for room five twenty.

Boysie could identify Ada's voice in the tiny trapped squawk that came from the instrument.

"Mostyn here." Curt. "Are you all in the building? . . . Good. You are to come down to Mr Oakes' room. Three ten . . . Yes, all of you and now."

The instrument clattered back into place.

"They're armed, I gather." To Boysie.

"Yes, but I doubt if they'd hit the Albert Hall from the Memorial."

"That could be hazardous." Mostyn did not smile. "You tooled up?" To Griffin.

"Fully clothed."

Mostyn holstered his automatic. The African by the door had done the same. "What're you carrying?" Mostyn asked Boysie, who told him.

"Where the hell did you get them from? You running a personal arms factory?"

"You should talk about arms factories."

"I am not going to tell you again, Oakes."

Mostyn leaned against the chairback. His poise transmitting arrogance: the tilt of his head, the manner in which his foot rested, the toe of his shoe touching the floor, heel raised. "I do not involve myself with illegality unless there is good reason. Money is not good reason, though, in the early stages of this particular operation, I had to intimate that it was. I do not dabble in illegal armaments deals." He turned to the man by the door. "Dacre." The African straightened up. "The gentleman over there is called Griffin. He is very good. As good as you. Griffin and yourself are responsible for the safety of the ladies. Understood?"

"Understood," mumbled Dacre.

"Mr Oakes comes with me."

"Where?" Boysie did not budge.

"To the heart of the matter, lad. To the hurricane's eye and the still centre of the whirlpool."

"What about me?" Snowflake Brightwater was on her feet.

"Eyes of hurricanes and still centres of whirlpools are not for the likes of you." Mostyn hardly paused for breath.

"Rotting, scavenged corpses." It was the worst exclamation she could muster.

"Obscenity will get you nowhere." Mostyn allowed his lips to slide into a smile. "You are a lady. Only the brave deserve you, the fair. Stay with the others and you will all be prizes for the victors."

For once Snowflake Brightwater seemed deflated. "Be brave, both of you."

"Courage is relative," sneered Mostyn.

The streets were busy. The sun did not shine but the air was wet with heat: a damp that stuck to the face and hands, penetrated clothing, drawing moisture from the body.

"Africa." Mostyn sniffed. "The whole continent in ferment, or coming up to the simmer. Democracy, communists, fascists, national socialists. You name them. Ferment. Guerrillas; plot; ploy; counterploy."

"You're talking poetry again." Boysie fell into step beside him. "I don't understand poetry."

"And you shouldn't be here. I used you in London because I thought the stink of money would keep your nose to the grindstone. You were a front, an exterior. I let you know a little more—like seeing that the aircraft were carrying arms—in case anything happened to me."

They pushed their way up the jostling pavement. Boysie noticed how Mostyn even walked in a ruthless manner, shouldering his way through the throng.

"I still don't read you straight."

"This tract; this parcel; this bloody rain and heat-ridden segment of land once belonged to the Empire, son. It was part of the far flung. Then we told them to go it alone and they did very well. But the country is restless. The roots are shallow. To put it in a small, hard, round, nutshell, we are on the lip of a coup."

They were crossing the Square of the Assembly, dodging the stream of late afternoon traffic. There seemed to be a steady flow of people in and out of the tall office block which Mostyn identified as the recently completed Government Administration Building. The people's dress was mainly European. Only here and there did one see the flash of colour denoting national costume.

"A coup, you said." They reached the far sidewalk in front of the low elegant House of Assembly.

"A coup d'état?"

Mostyn nodded. "The country is small: disseminated. He who commands this capital commands the country. Ideal for one overblown human with stunted political ideals, and ambition where his balls should be."

"Where do you fit?"

"The country has a treaty with Great Britain. We would not care for a fascist military dictatorship. Nor would we want to be embroiled in a tiny African Vietnam, even though the politics would be different. We prefer a bloodless counter coup."

"Who's doing the couping?"

"The big man? General Bushway. General *Elijah* Bushway would you believe? Trouble is that he hasn't even got half the army behind him. Had to call in mercenaries. He's even got a mercenary military commander."

"Colonel Peter Suffix?"

"You're with me."

"And who gets couped?"

"The gentleman we are going to see now. President Anthony."

"When?"

"Around six tonight. He's throwing a shindig, President

Anthony that is. Event of the season; everyone will be there. You wouldn't want to miss that, would you?"

"It depends."

"On what?"

"On how much shooting there's going to be and who's getting shot at."

They left the camp on foot, marching in file. Suffix rode in the first of the three Land-Rovers which brought up the rear of the column. Suffix's Land-Rover was identical with the British Special Air Service vehicles built for use on intruder missions. It had an armed position forward for two general purpose machine guns on a coupled mounting, and a third at the driver's position. In the rear was a mounted Browning machine gun.

Almost half of the men still had to collect their weapons and ammunition from Alaki Barracks.

When they reached the main road the fifteen heavy duty trucks were drawn up ready to receive them.

The men moved quickly: there was no bunching, pushing or talking. Their drill was impeccable.

Suffix's driver slewed the Land-Rover to the head of the convoy and they drove off, unhurried towards Otuka.

The hallway of the president's residence was gay with flowers. They rose in banks up the ornamented staircases which swept away on each side of the great oak doors leading to the reception room. The air inside felt fresh and cool, scented from flowers. For a second, Boysie reflected understanding for General Bushway. In this kind of climate the head man got to live in good conditions.

There were flowers in the reception room also. The floor was oak parquet, highly polished; a long room, stretching the depth of the house, the far wall being a huge window which looked out onto the garden. Boysie could see two Shea trees set close together, their branches almost touching.

The walls were hung with examples of Etszikan paintings: bold colours in abstract designs, beautiful primitive work.

To the right and left two doors led off the reception room to the main body of the house. The president and his party entered through the far left hand door.

The president smiled and stretched out his hand to Mostyn.

"Ah, you are welcome, my good friend. Is this the man you spoke of? Mr Oakes?"

Boysie shook the president's hand, bowing his head, a trifle bewildered at events.

"I think you know my son," President Anthony stepped back. "He is the chief of my Government Security Corps and has recently been on attachment to London."

"H-hi there, m-m-man. G-good t-to ha-have you with us." Mr Colefax grinned.

Boysie shuffled his feet and President Anthony returned his attention to Mostyn. "All is prepared, but I am sad, my son will not allow me to watch, or take part in, the final act."

"It will be better that you are kept safe." There was understanding in Mostyn's voice. "I know how you feel though, Mister President."

A tall Etszikan police officer had come into the room, he stood at attention obviously waiting to speak. President Anthony gestured to him.

"A crowd is starting to gather outside, Mister President: to watch the arriving guests."

The president turned to Mostyn and raised his eyebrows in question.

"Clear them. You'd better start clearing the streets now as well." He glanced at his watch. "It is almost time to receive the guests. Come Boysie, we have work to do."

Already they could hear the police loudhailers at work outside, sweeping civilians from the square and main streets of the city.

14

It had been a long day for General Bushway. He was conscious of his impatience. Not simply the impatience of this day, but the urgency and irritation which had built inside him through the years. Government by committee meant time wasted in endless argument and wrangling. Here, the wrangling was often protracted. This in itself was unbearable. Particularly when he could see the correct solutions so clearly.

He looked out from his office window onto the parade ground where his men were already lining up to embark in the lorries.

All day the activity had been kept to the minimum, now the General was beginning to see his force unleashed. The mercenaries, and specially trained insurgents, would arrive soon. Then they would drive in triumph into Otuka. Within the next few hours he would come face to face with Anthony. After that . . .

Colonel Impato completed his round of inspection: the Hotel Europa; the post office; the Government Administration Building; the House of Assembly and the radio and television stations. He now made one last call at the president's residence.

Mostyn stood in the hall with Boysie and a dozen members of the Etszikan Police Force.

From behind the doors leading to the reception room came the familiar buzz and clatter of a social gathering getting into stride.

"We're ready as you can hear," said Mostyn.

"I'm still not convinced." Boysie looked troubled. "What if they try a fire fight?"

"My men have the advantage." In spite of the words, Impato's voice struck a nervous key.

"Out there, maybe. I'm talking about in here."

"In here you pray," said the Colonel.

Suffix's force arrived at Alaki Barracks a few minutes after six. The General's troops were already embarked in their trucks and Suffix took the opportunity of making himself known to all the men: moving from truck to truck, staying a minute or so with each load while the unarmed men of his force were provided with weapons.

For convenience they had split the total force into two waves. Tilitson and Knox were to lead the first wave, taking charge of the radio and television station; cordoning off the Square of the Assembly, and occupying the Government Administration Building and House of Assembly before Tilitson carried on to the seaboard to take over the post office and the Europa Hotel.

The second wave would follow ten minutes after the first: the hundred picked men, led by Suffix and the General, who would go straight to the president's residence.

The General came out of his office block, tossing his pistol lanyard round his bull neck. He looked big, magnificent and unbeatable, in combat suit, his peaked cap at a rakish angle.

Suffix saluted. The General put a hand to his cap then extended it, his great paw enveloping Suffix's hand.

"It has arrived then."

"Yes, General. Good luck."

The first lorries started up.

"Permission to leave, sir." Tilitson stood at attention a few yards from the General.

"Go with speed. Be resolute. You act for this country and a new, enlightened, régime."

Suffix turned away. The General's political and melodramatic statements made him uneasy.

Tilitson saluted and doubled off to his jeep.

Motors roared and the first trucks began to move through the gates.

Colonel Impato viewed the area through his binoculars. From his vantage point on the roof of the Government Administration Building, he could overlook the key positions. He even had a view over the House of Assembly into the Square of Independence, where a large number of cars, belonging to members of the government and leading figures of state, were parked before the president's residence. He tightened the focus and ran the binoculars along the front of the residence. Six police officers stood at ease, guarding the entrance.

He swung the binoculars down to the square below. Quiet and normal.

The roof itself was like a fortress. A machine gun at each corner, and two more angled in on the roof entrance in the unlikely event of anyone getting past the precautions below them, in the building itself.

There was a chatter from the radio and Impato turned. His radio operator was crouched behind him. The operator acknowledged the call and looked up at Impato.

"They're just coming into the city, sir." Impato nodded grimly and loosened his automatic in its leather holster.

The radio and television station was a small squat building: pinkish concrete stapled with aerials, standing alone on a patch of dark open ground. In the main entrance there was a reception desk. Two corridors led off to a pair of small broadcasting studios, on one side, and one cramped television studio on the other.

Knox was in the first jeep. He had one truck with twenty men behind him. They came in fast from the main road, the vehicles slewing up dark dust as they pulled to a halt in front of the building.

Two men stayed by the entrance, their automatic rifles at the ready. Not a sound from inside. One minute. Two minutes. They were unprepared for their comrades to reappear, backing out of the building, hands raised, their weapons gone. Just as unprepared for the movement to their left and right. Two squads of army men coming round

177

the side of the building holding them in danger of utterly destructive crossfire.

Knox had been totally unready. Instead of the shirt-sleeved technicians and broadcasters he had expected, his party had suddenly been confronted by rifles and automatic weapons: in front, behind, suddenly appearing from door-ways.

A tall black officer gave the command. "Drop your weapons and nobody will get hurt."

One by one they obeyed.

"Now back out of the main door and try nothing: my men are outside and have you covered. One move and you all get it."

An army sergeant checked the truck. Bushway's men were searched and bundled into the vehicle. Nobody bothered about rank. There were two machine guns trained on the truck. The other men who had been waiting inside and around the building now took up defensive positions. Inside, the technicians and broadcasters remained off the air as ordered.

Impato's binoculars picked up the trucks before they reached the Square of the Assembly. There was a jeep in front with a white officer sitting next to the driver. The convoy growled into the square, men leaping from the trucks.

Two groups peeled off: one, headed by the white officer, going straight for the Government Administration Building; the other for the House of Assembly.

The remainder busied themselves in sealing off the entrances to the square. Impato smiled to himself. Below him, the coup was already being prevented. The clatter of men's boots on the square's hard surface floated upwards.

It felt like a routine exercise as they pulled into the square. Tilitson was proud of the smart, fast way his men worked. The minimum orders needed to be given. He felt elated as he ran up the steps of the Administration Building, his mind already picturing the surprise and panic of the civilian personnel caught unawares in the offices: all those little dolly spade girls. They worked late in the Administration Building.

Tilitson went straight across the foyer to the lifts. One sergeant, two men and himself. He could already hear the remainder of the detachment crashing up the stairs. The two men at reception stood against the wall, hands raised, looking frightened. Tilitson pressed the button for the top floor. Number six. The lift gradually rose.

None of Impato's men went into action until the whole unit was inside the building. On the ground floor they leaped from the doorways and hiding places. One of the five men left in the main hall whirled and fired at the movement coming from a door, but the bullet went wild, smashing into the concrete wall at the same moment as its instigator was sent spinning across the marble floor by a rip of automatic fire; a slippery trail of blood snaking over the floor behind him.

As Tilitson's men arrived at offices on the other floors they were met by the sudden appearance of troops, out-flanking and outgunning them. Not a civilian in sight for the building had been quietly cleared during the late afternoon.

The lift hummed upwards, indicator lights picking off the floors. Four . . . Five . . . Six. It stopped with a thud and the doors hissed open.

Tilitson stared into the barrel of a GPMG. From some-where else in the building there was a shot.

Tilitson reacted, his hand streaking out towards the operating button of the lift. His fingers were two inches from the *Down* button when the short burst ripped into the lift. They felt nothing, nor did they smell the cordite. The ten or so bullets, fired at close range, left the impression that a small grenade had exploded in the lift, the bodies were so torn by metal.

In the House of Assembly things did not go without incident. Sergeant Umata, a regular soldier with ten years' service, was in charge of a machine gun unit stationed directly in front of the president's chair—a big carved oak throne—in the main Chamber of the House.

A squad of ten men, each wearing Suffix's cobra symbol on the shoulder of his combat suit, threw open the doors to the Chamber and Umata shouted at them to stop. One insurgent was too fast, getting off three shots before Umata's unit could open fire. The second bullet caught Umata in the throat. He died later that evening in the Otuka General Hospital.

The young officer reported to Colonel Impato, on the roof, that all insurgent troops in the building were under control.

Within two minutes there was a radio message from the House of Assembly indicating a similar situation.

Impato motioned the men on the roof to be ready. Raising his loudhailer to his mouth he directed it towards the square where Bushway's men stood ready at the road blocks.

"This is Colonel Impato, Commander of the Army of Etszika."

One of the men at the north end of the square turned sharply, shading his eyes. Then his rifle came up. A machine gun burst tore from the roof, knocking the man over and splaying him out like a dummy.

"Your mission has failed," Impato continued. "Your comrades are either dead or under close escort. You are covered from all sides. I suggest you throw your weapons into the middle of the square and place your hands above your heads."

Slowly they began to move and, as the pile of rifles and automatic weapons grew, Impato's men started to emerge into the soft evening light.

Suffix did not like it. There were no people on the streets. No police or traffic. But perhaps that was simply the result of the first wave. They were moving at speed, coming right into the city now. He noticed that General Bushway, sitting behind him in the Land-Rover, was frowning.

"I've lost contact with Mr Tilitson's force, sir." From the radio operator.

The Land-Rover, leading five truckloads of troops, turned into the Square of Independence. Here there was a more normal scene. The four or five lines of big, polished motor cars parked in front of the residence. Police at the door.

Bushway groped on the floor for the loudhailer as they pulled up, the troops leaping out, going to their places without waiting for orders.

One of the policemen drew his revolver, but Bushway had already started to speak.

"You know me. General Bushway: Commander of the Army. I am here on government business. You will assist my troops."

The policeman returned his revolver to its holster. They stood aside while Bushway and Suffix, escorted by some ten men, ran up the steps and through the entrance.

In the hall, Bushway drew his revolver. Suffix followed suit. From behind the reception room doors came the noise of a party in full flood.

Bushway took a deep breath and placed his hands on the doorknobs.

"Right," he shouted, throwing the doors open and striding into the room.

They were carried forward by the momentum of their first steps, taking three paces into the room before coming to a halt.

In the centre of the reception room was a table. On the table stood a large tape recorder linked to four loudspeaker units placed near the doors. From the loudspeakers came the noises of cheerful revelry.

At the far end of the room, alone, sat Boysie Oakes sipping a large brandy.

"Nice of you to drop in." Boysie grinned.

"I know you." Suffix's voice echoed against the noise from the tape. "You're that bloody fool Oakes."

15

THE LIGHT WAS dimming in the square outside: a grey-out, grainy in texture, silence and tension almost splitting the eardrums. The scrape of a boot; the clank of a weapon against concrete.

Suffix's picked men ringed the front of the residence, statue still, at the ready: great, black aggressive shapes who could spit fire and death at a couple of centimetres squeeze in their forefingers.

The police had moved to one side. They watched the residence, keeping their eyes purposefully away from the ranks of polished parked cars. The car doors were opening: slowly, without noise.

They came from the interiors of the vehicles like cats. Chosen personally by Colonel Impato, shod in rubber-soled shoes, wearing combat suits and helmets, unhung with any extra equipment: they fanned out, away from the cars in which they had been hidden, creeping softly in towards their victims.

The final assault was as silent as the first appearance of Impato's ghost squad. In a last scurry they came up behind the stationary insurgents, choosing their individual quarries, homing in to prod their backs with sub-machine gun or automatic muzzles, or to prick the necks, in line with the jugular vein: knife points against flesh.

Suffix's men were in no position to argue. One by one weapons clattered to the ground. There were similar noises coming from the side and back of the residence where the same action was being taken.

The police joined in the job of herding Suffix's men into the centre of the square, away from the collected pile of weapons. The tension had begun to ease, though four of Impato's men crouched ready, near the door of the residence.

The strain returned for a second with the echo of the first shot from deep inside the house.

In the reception room the moment was frozen. Suffix and Bushway inside the door; their ten men, bewildered, behind them; the blare from the tape; Boysie leaning back on his chair.

One of the doors, to the side, on the right, opened and Mostyn walked coolly into the room. He crossed to the tape recorder and banged down the *Stop* key.

"That's better. One can hear oneself think now. I suggest you drop your weapons, you are covered from behind."

A dozen Etszikan soldiers had insinuated themselves through the doors and were beginning to prod Bushway and Suffix's bodyguards out of the room.

Suffix looked round at the sound of movement. He shrugged and let his pistol drop. It hung, swinging like a lazy pendulum from its lanyard.

Bushway stood unmoving. Mostyn altered his position slightly so that the muzzle of his automatic could be seen above the tape recorder. The doors behind Bushway and Suffix were closed.

"The gun, General." Mostyn's bark had a bite sharp enough to cause the African a quick reflex. His pistol dropped on its lanyard, dangling at his knees.

Boysie carefully put down his glass: fingers shaking. He removed his left hand from the inside of his jacket, revealing the stubby Diamondback which he transferred to his right hand before standing up.

"Oh, what trouble you have caused," said Mostyn.

"By what right . . . ?" began Suffix, then he changed his mind. "I suppose you're a gunboat?"

Mostyn smiled. "Something of the sort. Troubleshooter they call it these days. Americanism, but a vivid word—troubleshooter." He rolled it, savouring the word's flavour. "You're in trouble, comrade Suffix. How many sides have you got to your coat?"

"I'm apolitical. Just a hireable blunt instrument and a military brain."

Bushway slowly turned his large head. "I demand to see President Anthony."

"You'll see plenty of President Anthony before you're through." Boysie had moved up to Mostyn. Where the hell was Colefax, he thought. They had promised to come down and take this pair off their hands once the square and residence were cleared.

Mostyn walked up to Suffix, standing directly in front of him. Boysie was behind Mostyn's left shoulder.

The clanking of the fans; Bushway sweating: a tic tightening in Suffix's cheek, a coiling of the muscles. Boysie should have diagnosed the symptoms; Mostyn certainly should have recognised them: a man under pressure, curling, tightening himself for action.

When he did move, Suffix went like some beautifully precisioned piece of machinery. Both hands flashed up together. The left palm jabbing Mostyn in the chest, sending him sliding backwards on the polished floor. The right palm went sideways, catching Bushway's shoulder. The General going with the push, his feet slipping, the heavy body falling.

In the stranded second, Boysie got a lot of images. Suffix shouting "General!" Mostyn's face, a blur of shock as he slithered back. Bushway's eyes flicking sharply: left, right, left, right, right. The head turning. The pistol on the lanyard. Suffix's boots on the oak floor, thudding. His hand drawing up his lanyard as he made for the door.

The Diamondback came up. Boysie felt the kickback and saw wood splintering from the door as Suffix jerked at the handle: the door to Boysie's right.

Mostyn shouting: "Boysie. Bushway."

The great black hand closing over the pistol on the floor. The thump of Mostyn's automatic and he fired from a sitting position behind Boysie.

Bushway's scream as the bullet ripped and shattered the General's shoulder.

"Get Suffix. Stop him, Boysie. Go, Boy . . ." Mostyn

yelling as though to a dog, on his feet again now and leaping for the groaning General: not to offer aid but to get the lanyard from around his neck.

Boysie felt the vague tremor of unnatural worry behind the gout of anxiety in his stomach. He was sliding and jumping towards the door, stupidly concerned that he did not know the geography of the building.

Through the door a passage ran at right angles. The noise of Suffix's feet to the right, out of sight, round the sharp corner, going left. Boysie felt Mostyn behind him.

"This way."

"Careful at the corner, Boysie."

Boysie skidded to a halt and jabbed his gun barrel out from the wall's angle.

Nothing.

Mostyn was carrying two guns, his own and Bushway's pistol. There were more feet behind them, coming down the passage. Colefax and two men.

"Bushway. Wounded in the reception room," Mostyn shouted.

Colefax veered towards the room, one of his companions yelled that the passage led to the garden.

Boysie jumped from the angle of the wall. There was a short length of passage and then another corner, right angled, going right. As he began to move there was a shot from behind the corner and the sound of breaking wood.

Boysie dug his heels in, braking, but he was moving too fast. He rounded the corner, putting out his hand to steady himself against the far wall.

In front, a door with the latch blown off, pushed open. Through the door, the darkening garden, part-lit from the lights of the residence. Going like some priest-pursued devil was the shape of Suffix, pounding across the lawn.

Boysie leaned against the door jamb. Heart pumping, a tightening of the forehead, chest heaving, he lifted his arm and aimed over the foresight. He could still see Suffix. Squeeze. The kick. Explosion. Acrid smell. Shot went left, he had felt himself pull away. Left hand up, closing over the right. Steadying. Suffix almost blurred now, merging with the night.

Squeeze again. High.

Suffix leaping into the air and disappearing into a dark clump fifty or sixty yards away.

Right ear slammed by the noise of Bushway's pistol in Mostyn's hand crashing twice.

To the right, outside, there was some kind of patio with a stone seat. Boysie heaved himself towards it, hitting the dirt, as he heard the thump of a bullet into the wall above. He had the impression of a flash from where Suffix disappeared. Round the corner of the seat, he pointed at where the flash had been and fired twice.

Mostyn was beside him, huddled behind the seat.

Two more flashes and bullets punching, tearing into the doorway they had vacated. Mostyn put one round in the direction of the flashes.

Boysie tried to do some quick arithmetic to see how many rounds he had left. But the brain would not work. He felt in his pocket, removing the box of cartridges, flicking open the chamber, ejecting and reloading in the dark.

Mostyn breathed hard beside him. "Bleeder's over there. Wish to hell they'd get some lights going."

Boysie grunted. Then. "Hey, Frobisher and Pesterlicker?"

"What about Frobisher and Pesterlicker?"

Two more shots from across the black garden. Mostyn fired once.

"Who are they?" Boysie flinched at the pistol shot.

"Who did they say they were?"

Boysie finished reloading and closed the chamber. It made a solid reassuring click.

Another flash and a ricochet very close. Boysie sighted carefully on the flash, held in his mind, and fired twice.

"They said they were Investigation Branch: Ministry of Transport and Civil Aviation."

"Then that's who they were."

"But Colefax said he was Investigation Branch. Ministry of Transport."

"Prove he wasn't."

"Your people?"

"Could be, Oaksie, could be. Where're those bloody lights?"

"And who are you these days?"

"At the moment I represent HM Government. The Foreign Office."

There seemed to be a hiss as the lights came on. A spreading flood of illumination from the garden arcs.

For a second they were both blinded by it, then Boysie saw him, silhouetted on the garden wall not sixty feet from them. Both their hands came up, but before they could fire there was a rip of sub-machine gun burst from above.

Suffix appeared to be lifted into the air, spinning like a humming top.

Their ears still sang from the noise of the sub-machine gun, but the crunch, as Suffix fell back onto the top of the wall, was clearly audible. He flopped over the stone, then, hesitating, dropped with a double thud into the garden.

Looking up, Boysie saw Mr Colefax leaning from an upper window, a Sterling sub-machine gun protruding. Mr Colefax was smiling.

"That's the Board of Trade for you," said Mostyn.

"What coup d'état, darlings?" asked Snowflake Bright-water. "We know nothing of a coup d'état."

"We have been playing strip poker with your friends," added Ada.

"Yes, we stripped and they . . ." Aida grinned, she was hanging on to the arm of Dacre who looked a happier man.

"All velly ingenious." Alma had an inscrutable smile going.

"I heard some shooting but didn't like to worry the girls." Griffin grinned.

"There are still one or two things . . ." Boysie turned to Mostyn.

"All in good time, laddie, all in good time."

"You set up this whole deal to knock out a coup?"

"To puncture a *putsch*." Mostyn's eyes narrowed. "I set

it up on instructions. Averted a full scale fight-in and HMG is not involved."

"But you went to all the trouble of . . ."

"The idea was put to me in the first place. Think, lad, think. We'll see him when we get to London anyway. The fellow who fingered your old man. You with me?"

Boysie's brow crinkled.

Mostyn pressed the bell at the door of the mews flat and they waited. It was ten o'clock in the morning, four days later, and they had come straight from Heathrow: a warm morning with sunshine painting the streets. London bright.

Nobody replied to the first ring so Mostyn pressed again.

After a minute there was a shuffling from inside. A bolt being drawn back. The door opened and a fat lady clad in carpet slippers, with a jazzy apron over her dress, was revealed.

"Yes?" As though she was afraid they wanted money.

"We've come to see the Admiral." Condescension dripping from Mostyn's lips.

"He's gone." She pronounced it 'gorn'.

"Where?" Icily.

"South Africa. Yesterday. Unexpected. Left me a note. I clean for him."

"I see. May we come in for a moment?"

She looked uncertain so Mostyn dug his hand in his pocket and presented her with a piece of plastic. Boysie tried to get a glimpse but failed.

The fat lady was impressed by what she read on the piece of plastic.

Mostyn led the way into the small sitting room where they had drunk champagne on the foundation of Air Apparent. Nothing had changed.

"Sly bugger." Mostyn looked around.

"You mean the Chief?"

"Who else?"

"Not the Chief."

"Drunken old bastard." Mostyn was annoyed. "Yes, of course the Chief. I mean it. He's always been a bit of a fascist. Covered it by saying he was true blue, but the seeds were always there. Brain a bit gone with drink, but he was still agile. He moved pretty sharpish. South Africa."

"How did you find out?"

"He came to the wrong man, didn't he?"

"You?"

"He brought me the blueprint of Air Apparent. More or less the same way that I brought it to you, only he named names and places. One of the places was Otuka. He knew exactly how to fix the landings and refuellings. He had a lot of contacts. Making a fortune out of the arms deals. I, being who I am, took the whole parcel to the Foreign Office. They already knew about Bushway and his plot. They also knew Suffix was in town with a shopping list. In the end they gave me a team and told me to get on with it. I came to you."

"Bloody hell." Boysie scratched his head. "You can never tell with people, can you?"

"I'm sorry he's gone. For your sake."

"My sake?"

Mostyn crossed the room to where the Chief's old souvenir photographs hung. He unhooked one and passed it to Boysie.

The Chief, a good deal younger, sat in the centre. He was in uniform and flanked by some fifteen or sixteen younger men in civilian clothes. The printed caption read *Admiralty I Department (Europe) 1936.* Boysie looked blankly.

"Recognise anyone, lad?"

He shook his head. "Only the Chief."

"Look at the gentleman third from his left."

Across the years Commander Robert Oakes looked out of the faded picture at his son.

"Jesus."

"He knew." Tight lipped, unusual for Mostyn. "One night, oh a couple of years after you joined the Department, he was in his cups. He told me you looked like your father."

"Sod it. Sod it." Boysie held the picture towards Mostyn.

"Keep it. For old times' sake keep it."

Boysie's hand came up and the photograph spun viciously

towards the wastepaper basket. "I don't want the bloody thing. I want to work. Get on with it. Clear the bastards out. I don't want to think about it any more and if you ever mention it to me again, Mostyn, I'll do you. I'll bloody do you."

Mostyn nodded. "One thing," he said. "If he does come back, I shall have to tell you first."

"You do that. You bloody well do that."

GRACE NOTE

ONE WEEK LATER. Summer. London. Boysie's flat. Early evening.

He came out of the bathroom, whistling and expectant. Dinner with Snowflake Brightwater with no dramas or impending dramas. He smelled of *Aramis* and looked healthily smart. The brown double-breasted; a cream shirt and gold tie.

Boysie straightened his tie and shot his cuffs. The doorbell rang.

It was Alma, looking lovely but sheepish.

"Hallo, dark oriental beauty."

Alma blushed. She had always been the most shy of the three girls.

"I have come to confess, to give and to share my winnings." She slunk into the room.

"Confess?"

"Ada and Aida. They had cards, yes."

"Yes."

"Which you signed?"

"Yes." It was Boysie's turn to feel sheepish. "But they're destroyed. They each came to me last week. Took their cards, then brought them back the next day. They burned them here."

"I have come to burn my card."

"You didn't have a card. We didn't . . ."

Alma held up a plain white card. Her name was typed in the top left hand corner. In the centre was Boysie's signature and a date.

"I didn't sign that. I . . ."

"No. I am a good forger. Wily oriental trick. You see,

Boysie, we all thought you were a lovely man and fancied you. You're a dolly gent. There was an argument so we agreed to have a sweepstake. It came to fifty pounds. It was to go to the one who made you first. Closing date last week. I fancied you like mad but I am very shy."

"I noticed."

"So I simply performed forgery. Two days after we started the sweepstake. Last week we all produced our cards and I won the fifty quid." She smiled. "I am still shy, but my conscience pricks."

"You want to share the loot?"

"Yes. And give you the pleasure you deserve. It would be very pleasurable for me also."

"Keep the loot," smiled Boysie.

Remembering that you never look a gift horse and all that, he picked up the telephone and dialled.

"Hi," he said when Snowflake answered. "Can you keep dinner warm for me, love, I've got something needs doing straight away . . . Oh, a couple of hours . . . Good girl.'